Where

Wicked

Starts

Where Wicked Starts

a novel

Elizabeth Stuckey-French
and Patricia Henley

LACEWING BOOKS
INDIANAPOLIS

Lacewing Books
an imprint of Engine Books
PO Box 44167
Indianapolis, IN 46244
lacewingbooks.org

Printed in the United States of America

10   9   8   7   6   5   4   3   2   1

ISBN: 978-1-938126-26-0

Library of Congress Control Number: 2014944274

*All things truly wicked start
from innocence.*

ERNEST HEMINGWAY

Chapter 1

NICK

My snakeskin flats skim and skim some more, gritty against the sidewalk. I feel so good I don't feel fat.

It's the start of Christmas break and something awesome has finally happened. At Caroline Rex's house, six ninth grade girls pretended they didn't want the ton of cookies they ate and exchanged presents. Maeve Murphy got mine—Candy Cane body wash. I got a silver shoe pendant, perfect for me, since I own seventeen pairs of flats. Caroline lives on the canal in a house Dad would call "uptown." He means that they are not in a constant state of renovation. In the backyard, Caroline has a pool shaped like a teardrop. She has three dogs, not a slobberer among them. Her father showed us a few dog tricks. One could dance in a circle on his hind legs. It was good until Caroline's mother came home with a new tat on her arm: a sleeve of Gerber daisies. We had to gather around and act like it mattered to us. Tattoos seem like stupid parent crap now; I wouldn't get one if you paid me. I walk home through Skeeter, where the houses are close together and friendly-looking, with oil drum barbecues in the muddy front yards and a po' boy sandwich store at one corner. Girls on one block skip rope, double Dutch. *Alligator, alligator, I can't swim—*

In the faded Florida sunshine, I sing to myself: *At last. I'm in.*

A hammer in his hand, Dad squats on the derelict, slanting front porch of Sha-Na-Na Bed and Breakfast (what I call "the B") in a t-shirt with a leering pirate on the front. He always has a hammer in his hand. "Hey, pumpkin."

"Don't call me that."

"Sugar pie. Sweetheart. Cuddle bunny."

"Dad."

He says something that sounds like, "Goo-goo T?" He's hammering now, oblivious. I know he means, "You have a good time?" I could probably say, "I broke my arm today," or "I failed a test," and he wouldn't really pay attention.

"It was okay." No way would I give up my grudge about moving to Coquina Bay. What my stepsister Luna calls "Cock-in-a Bay." She can turn anything into an obscenity. And when my grudge against Dad slaps my heart, other, older grudges come to life. I'm only fourteen—the word *grudge* is new to me. I like it. My therapist Louise says that it's a way to explore what I feel. She says grudges are like a trip we take. She wants me to go down every little street and alley of my grudge until I know it the way I know my own face. Here's a grudge for you: Dad locked me in my room after my mother died. I couldn't sleep for like a year, so at night he'd lock me in. To keep me from wandering the house, he said. To protect me from myself.

"Kat's at the grocery," he says. He and Kat make a big deal about saying where she is *at all times*. They want Luna and me to do the same. But I know we won't. Luna goes before me, forging the way. I'm coming into the secret times, when I will lie and deliberately forget what I want to keep from them. My mother speaks to me— sort of from the grave—and she says to tell the truth. But Luna says that lying is how you become who you are.

Dad hammers hard. My signal to go indoors.

The foyer of the B has an echo and a ghost. The echo is a warble of your voice when you holler, "Anybody home?" And the ghost is a swish of cold air that wraps around your ankles, like craven claws. Only Luna and I believe in the ghost, and I only half-believe it. The stairs creak; I take them two at a time.

In the upstairs hallway, I call out, "Luna?" I want to somehow inform her that I'm *in*.

No Luna. No big sister. No stepsister. No tormenter. No cray-cray girl in the next bedroom. No girl to envy. No girl to idolize. All the things she is to me. I am alone in the house—who knows for how long? I can just be happy for a little while. I like to have a novel going, but I don't. I'm on a Neil Gaiman kick and finished *Stardust* yesterday. What to do? I can reorganize my collection of flats or I can play Words with Friends or I can try on my secret underwear and pretend to take a nap and for that I need a locked door.

The door I open to something amiss.

An unfamiliar oily smell—like a spice—seeps into my nose. I go to my flats tucked in the canvas shoe organizer hanging on the closet door. My Betsy Johnsons with the red patent toecaps, my one pair of precious Tieks, off-brands from Target and Walmart: all there. Inside the closet are shelves off to the side, deep to the right, that you might not even know were there since the closet light doesn't work. It's a stick-on LED light that must have died out a long time ago. Kat calls the tile on the closet floor shit-brown. I shove aside my clothes on the hangers and slip inside. I pretend I'm blind. It smells a little like the Goodwill, like flakes of human skin and sweat. I feel around for my mother's wooden box on the shelf. Just to make sure it's there. I can't stand to open it. The box is carved with designs. I tap my fingers over the designs. The box seems like it's been moved slightly to the right. I know my room—okay? One thing I learned in Montessori school was to put things back and keep things neat. I move the box leftward and try to decide if someone has been in my closet. People mosey in and out of the B all day long—anyone could've done it. Dad and Kat have helpers of all sorts, cleaning people and workers—everyone helping to get us ready to open the doors to the public. Then we'll be completely stripped of our privacy. This closet is my privacy. My Easter basket with its crinkly cellophane grass still has candy in it. Kat doesn't believe in Easter baskets. She celebrates the Spring Equinox like all good pagans. "She's too old for a basket," she said last spring. And Dad said, "One more year." He stood up to her. Usually he doesn't. I am so sick of him saying *Darlin' this* and *Darlin' that* to Kat. In the closet, I slip into the candy trance, peeling little chocolate eggs of their foil, nibbling on stale jellybeans.

It might've been bliss, but I can't stop wondering if someone strange has been in my room. Or Luna. Who's strange, but not a stranger. Kat says my intuition works overtime. Dad says I don't need a Ouija board to know which way the wind blows.

"Caught you!" Luna squeals. My heart nearly thuds out of my chest.

She grabs my shirt and tugs me out of the closet. I run my sticky, chocolate-y fingers through her hair.

"You bitch!" she yells.

We tussle on the bed, but my heart isn't in it. I can talk tough, but I'm not a fighter, in spite of the karate classes Dad insisted on when I was little. We're huffing and puffing.

"You're a closet eater," she says. "Face it."

My blood boils. I understand what boiling blood feels like. "Get off my bed."

Luna stands up, but presses one knee on the edge of the bed, just to prove she can. Her jeans are ripped at the knee. You can see the faint purple of her bra through her white t-shirt. She has real breasts. She doesn't need a padded bra. Her nails are polished eggshell blue.

I bat her away, not quite slapping, but it might be interpreted as slapping. "Out, out, out! You came in without knocking!" I love her so much. She seems like a badass pop star, a diva, like someone on the cover of a magazine.

She wags her butt to the door, sing-songy, whispering, "Lardy lady, lardy lady…"

I hate my dad for introducing her to Queen. Before Luna met us she didn't know squat about rock and roll.

What a way to start Christmas break.

Luna is almost sixteen and I am right in the middle of being fourteen, a nothing age when what you're allowed to do can fit in a shoebox.

She doesn't have her license, but Luna can drive. Late at night Dad takes her to the empty mall parking lot and she does figure-eights and backing up in our family van. She wouldn't be caught dead in that van in daylight. To prepare us for adulthood, Kat made the whole family sit down and watch a video about not texting while driving. Kat is always coming up with things to prepare us for adulthood. Which might happen when I'm thirty, I'm thinking.

Luna keeps company with boys after dinner, even if they do have to undergo an embarrassing inspection by Kat. "I know what's on your mind," she always says to them. Or: "These are my girls and it's my job to protect them." She says *girls*—plural—to take away the sting. As if to say, "This is my general policy and has been for years and will be until kingdom come." Where is Dad during this inspection? Absent. Luna turns passion pink and hauls the guy off to the library where they play gin rummy for kisses, following a rule Kat said she had to follow when she was in high school: Keep the door ajar and your feet on the floor. Sometimes if I'm bored, I go outside and spy on them through the gauzy curtains, from a wrought-iron balcony that's an easy reach from the crape myrtle trees.

Kat has her rules. No TV in our rooms. No "electronic games" in the house. It would spoil the ambience of the B. *Ambience* is a word we hear a hundred times a day. Ambience is all about what our guests will want, comfort and little luxuries, but with a twist of rock and roll. Oh, they don't want true rock and roll; they want the *idea* of rock and roll, vintage posters of Jerry Lee Lewis and Little Richard. A soft rock CD like hypnotic wavelets in every room. If they wanted true rock and roll, they'd love to see Luna's tongue as it wraps disgustingly around the tongue of the boy-of-the-week. I'd never want to trade places, but I have to admit it's hot. *Hot* is something Dad and I pretend I know nothing about.

In the words of my therapist Louise, we are all in a "period of adjustment." Dad and Kat have been married for six months, and that makes Luna and me stepsisters. Kat says, "Someday you'll just say *sisters*." I doubt that, and I have doubted it, right from the day I saw Dad and Kat leaning toward each other in front of our old school in Tallahassee, as if they couldn't close the gap fast enough. Dad wore a Jacksonville Suns cap with a snarky looking sunshine on the front. He'd taken it off, like some courtly gentleman gesture, and he fiddled with the cap, rolling it around and around, while Kat stood on a stone step a little above him in a pink flyaway dress, the hem lifted this way and that by the breeze. I have a Sixth Sense about romance; I can smell it a mile away. After the serious, embarrassing family meetings, the wedding, schlepping the boxes and moving in with them, getting my own room—in the renovated garage in Kat and Luna's house in Tallahassee—after all that, not only did I doubt our blending potential, I was royally pissed at moving away from our old neighborhood. As if it didn't really matter that we had lived within two blocks of a comics shop where I could trade three for one. And a Gumby's pizza. And a food co-op where there was a peanut butter grinder you operated by riding a bicycle. I hadn't ridden the bicycle since I was a little kid, but it was a memory. *My* memory.

After we all moved in together, Kat just sort of took over.

She said it was appalling that I'd been sleeping without a top sheet on my bed. She took me to the mall and bought me a bed-in-a-bag set, polka-dot sheets, a comforter, and pillowcases. She whisked through my room with a smudge stick on fire, getting rid of the evil spirits, she said. A sage smell was left behind, like dirt. Behind my back, she sorted through my old clothes and gave them away when I wasn't looking. That was the first time I yelled at her. "Those are my *memories* you gave away!"

Sometimes I think she wants to erase my mother from our lives.

And then we made the big move. And here's the worst part. To move to Coquina Bay, Dad sold the record store that had been our second home since I was a baby. It had comfy chairs and a cat named Elvis. I grew up there, listening to Ray Charles and Brenda Lee and the Supremes.

All Dad and Kat think about is remodeling the Sha-Na-Na: tiles, paint chips, menus, business cards, joining the Coquina Bay Chamber, blah, blah, blah. Every tile and screw and gallon of paint paid for with my mother's life insurance money. Will there be any left for college? *My* college?

Luna and I are at Coquina Bay High, a squat, tan school like a bowling alley, not far from the beach. On windy days, sand blows in under the doors and piles up in the corners of the hallway. I feel shipwrecked there. People actually kid themselves and say it's a party school. Because it's near the beach. They scare me, they're so wild. Their eyes are smeared with make-up. They show off their belly button rings in the john. I catch Luna's eye in the hall sometimes and she looks like someone on her way to the guillotine, bug-eyed, shoulders hunched. Her diva-ness faded.

•

The morning after the chocolate-in-the-hair incident is December 23rd, the first full day of Christmas vacay. We aren't speaking to each other and Kat and Dad haven't even noticed.

At breakfast, we explore our options through Kat. We speak directly to her and she speaks to both of us. I want to go to a movie. Luna wants to go to the Alligator Farm and visit Nana Fanny. Luna has sort of adopted my Nana—she thinks she's cool. To me she's my grandmother—all I've got. (My other grandmother lives on an island near Seattle—almost another country. She sends me mushy cards and twenty-dollar bills for every holiday.)

Kat says, "How about a movie later?"

I roll my eyes. Later could mean next week.

To sweeten the deal, Kat says, "My treat."

Luna says, to Kat, "I have a photography assignment. The Alligator Farm is almost like homework."

Kat says, to me, "Doesn't Maeve What's-her-name live next door to Nana Fanny?"

How could she forget Maeve's last name? "Maeve *Murphy*," I say, snot and meanness dripping from my words.

I regret ever mentioning Maeve, a girl in my homeroom. Not because I don't like her, but I don't want Kat in my business. I am dying to see Maeve in her natural habitat, on her skateboard. She said that she usually skates after dark, to avoid the law. I am dying of curiosity about a girl who even thinks about avoiding the law. What other secrets does she have? So maybe she won't be skateboarding; maybe she'll just happen to be looking out the window and see us. Maybe she'll invite me to her house. Maybe we'll be instant friends. I love the sound of those two Ms—Maeve Murphy.

"Friendship is partly about proximity," Kat says. "Being available."

I refuse to make eye contact. So why does she always say her best friend lives in Arkansas?

Kat gives us ten dollars each and says, "There's more where

that came from. There *will* be a movie. There *will* be piles of goodies under the tree. Be sweet. Stay together." She can't wait to get rid of us.

We ride our bikes into a big chilly wind, across the Manatee Bridge all the way to the Alligator Farm. Still not speaking. Our neighbor Molly works at the Alligator Farm and she waves us inside without making us pay.

The alligators in the lagoon pile up like gigantic turds. Or slugs in Nana Fanny's garden. On the sly, as if I might be talking to myself, I say, "Turds, I tell you."

Luna says, "Don't be gross."

Seven words, total. It's a start. On the bike ride I had a change of heart. How can we go all of Christmas break without speaking? I think about how the alligators know nothing of holidays or girlfriends or retro rock. Or do they?

Luna has a pocketsize camera, and she takes pictures of monkeys and albino crocodiles and egrets, but not their whole selves. She has a thing about photographing body parts: a wing, a gnarly bird foot. Or with people: a wrinkled sunburned neck, a big toe. Her art teacher says she had a good eye for composition.

We aren't talking again so I drift off thinking about what I do almost every night when I go to bed. An impulse after watching Luna and some guy DFK-ing, my hand drifting under the elastic of my military-gray, Gap underpants. Fingers still buttery from day-old popcorn Dad left on the counter. The thought of that butter is tied like a knot with *what I do*. Oh, sure, I know there are words for it. My sex education began years ago, but Kat felt obligated to do her stepmotherly duty and tell me how the sperm gets to the egg. She used all the right words; she's clinical. But I can't say them. And I will double-die if I get caught and have to listen to Kat say the word. It's a feeling like sugar on your taste buds magnified a thousand times a thousand times a thousand.

The alligators, up close, seem to be smiling crookedly, happy to lounge all over each other like puppies. Molly, in khaki shorts and hiking boots, her smile as bright as sunshine, chirps into a microphone. Seriously. If any human can chirp, it's Molly. She says that alligators keep each other warm.

I don't like seeing animals penned up. I stopped eating anything that has a mother when I was eight-and-a-half. In my family I'm the only vegetarian. The rest of them are big-time carnivores and would eat alligator, goat, snake, and porcupine, as well as the usual smoked ribs. The Alligator Farm is for Luna, who takes every photo opportunity she can find. Down there on an island in the middle of the slimy-looking lagoon, Molly calls the alligators by name—Buck and Sugar and Sleepy and more, they all have names—and a guy who works there comes down with a bloody, dead rodent dangling from his hand. A nutria, Molly says. Nutrias were brought to Louisiana from South America, against their will, I'm certain. They have bright orange buckteeth like Dorito chips. They live in cozy families in dams, like beavers, making more nutria like crazy. Farmers hate them because they eat fields of rice and sugarcane. The alligators lunge and the guy drops the nutria into the open white mouth of the first alligator to reach him. We hear the crunch of rodent bones.

I don't know why humans feeding the nutria to alligators seems more repulsive to me than an alligator in the wild snagging a nutria and chomping on it, but it does. What's right and wrong keeps me awake at night.

The guy with the bucket reaches in for smaller, brownish critters. He tosses them into the open mouths of the alligators. The gators beat the lagoon water with their spiky tails.

I decide to whine. "Luna, let's get out of here." Both of us know that she's really in charge.

"Not yet," she says. "I want to get some secret shots."

She goes to a wooden bench and stands up on it. She aims the camera toward the onlookers at the other side of the lagoon.

People in vacation clothes, leaning on the bamboo fence posts. People with little kids on their shoulders. Monkeys cry out. Birds coo. Sunshine falls in globs around the lagoon. The day is *trying* to warm up. The sweep of her camera lens is so quick, so wide, that she could be taking pictures of trees or birds. But I'll see the secret shots later: that's the fun part.

Molly gazes at the rodent guy and I know for sure that she has a crush on him. Intuition revs up. I'm like a psychic. Weighed down with TMI. How can she like him after he handled the bloody, dead rodents? Kat says there's no accounting for chemistry when people fall in love. She should know. She and Luna don't have a single good thing to say about Luna's father.

I pace around the lagoon. Molly takes off her safari hat—her red hair fluffing in curls over her shoulders—and she tells the onlookers that when you turn fifteen, you are allowed to come down to the island and have your photo taken with alligators. Luna wants to do it; I never will.

The ten one-dollar bills feel suddenly spendable in my jeans pocket. Dry and bulky and spendable. The urge to spend the money grows as strong as the urge to leave. I consider—for a half-minute—spending it on a Christmas present for Dad. But he will have to make-do with the presents Luna and I bought together: a beaded beer-bottle opener and a Champion Dad baseball cap. At the snack bar I ask for popcorn, a Twix bar, and a Diet Sprite. At a picnic table, I eat sneakily. I don't want anyone to know how much I want to devour it all. I unbutton my jeans; they are a little tight. Palm trees rustle all around me, a soothing sound. Luna looks confident, taking photos. She doesn't like her nose and she hates her ankles. But there's a don't-mess-with-me tilt to her hip. To me, she's beautiful. She says the camera gives her a place to hide.

I watch the people, chocolate melting in my mouth. A man and a girl stand apart. He wears worn leather sandals, what Dad would call Jesus shoes. His hair is yellowish-white, in a long ponytail. They have no idea how close I am. I hear him say, "Bony," in a sly voice.

The girl definitely does not look like a "Bony." She's not fat, but she's not skinny. She might be thirteen, or she might be ten. I almost say the word *precocious* out loud, I like it so much. This man and this girl do not match. He looks like an ordinary dad, in wrinkled khakis and a tropical shirt. Her clothes are gorgeous in a slinky kind of way. Like a doll he dressed up in fishnet tights under a very short pleated skirt and a real leather bomber jacket. She glances up at him, cocking her head. I can't see her expression. But everything about her says, "I'm cute and I know it."

In a sneaky, gravelly voice, he says, "You'll get down in there with the alligators."

"I will?"

"You will. When you're fifteen. And he'll put his snout up against you."

As if to say he didn't mean it, the man slips his arm across her chest from behind and gathers her close, too close. He whispers something. He puts his mouth very close to her ear.

My Sixth Sense shouts: She's not his daughter.

Nana Fanny lives in a pink and white suburb on a creek, with egrets sleeping in the trees, white feathery blobs, like someone hung toilet paper as a Halloween prank. Lazily we ride our bikes through her sleepy neighborhood. Sunlight blazes on the houses. The houses seem empty and boring—all alike. Except for Nana Fanny's. Her front door is decorated with a quarter moon hammered out of metal. Like a witch's house, Kat said once.

We knock. I keep one eye out for Maeve Murphy, but her house looks closed up. Like maybe they've gone on vacay. While we wait, Luna says, "Did you see that girl?"

This is really the end of not speaking to each other. "I know who you mean."

"I got a shot of them."

"They didn't match." I do not want to picture them. The way he put his arm around her makes me anxious. Feeling anxious is like I'm waking up from a nightmare I can't escape. Like when my mother died.

Luna says, "It was sort of..."—her voice goes up to a squeak—"...creepy."

Nana Fanny opens the door and squeezes us close. She wears a sundress with a stretchy top under it: a sea blue dress with a sea green top. I roll my eyes at the dress, but not so that Nana Fanny can see. She tries too hard to be young. Her jewelry rattles. Her toenails are painted copper. She's plump and I wonder—did I inherit her plumpness? She has chin wattles: Kat told me what they're called. Wattles. They shiver when she talks and makes a point. Nana Fanny has many points to make. She has a life story that goes on and on. She's seventy. Her life story is like burrowing into the Internet to get the answer to one question and that answer leading you to another question and another. Her life has mistakes and sorrows. It has highs and lows. Heartaches. You have to tune her out. Dad probably always wanted an ordinary mother, not a poet—she writes poetry day and night—not a woman who would run off with a cruise ship chef when Dad was only seven years old. Not a woman who still wears a bikini and goes out to the beach to get a little sun once a week.

"Raspberry thumbprints are in the oven," she says, grinning, as if we're five years old. Her lipstick is a purplish stain and it bleeds a little into the wrinkles above her mouth. I try not to look at it.

Luna swings her camera by a strap. "I got some good shots," she says.

Nana Fanny says, "Oh, I can't wait."

We drop our backpacks on the floor. I put up one finger, my lifelong signal to Nana Fanny that I need to go to the bathroom. But once in the hallway, I slip into the guest room and behind the heavy drapes to stare at Maeve's house.

Maeve's backyard has a sculpture of a naked woman. And a *huge* doghouse. But no dog. Someone has draped a fringed shawl over the naked woman's shoulders.

There is a ruckus when Nana Fanny lets Haiku in the kitchen door. Haiku comes sniffing into the guest room, flipping and whimpering around my feet. Haiku is a Corgi, brown like peanut butter with eyes that make you love her. Reluctantly, I give up on Maeve Murphy.

Nana Fanny calls out, "Shall we have cookies first? And then see the secret shots?"

Haiku and I go back to the kitchen and eat cookies, speed-eating to get to Luna's photos. I feed Haiku under the table. My skin gets a tingly-crawly feeling that Kat says comes from too much sugar. Kat's voice is always needling in my head, even though I try to smother it. Sometimes I can't remember the sound of my own mother's voice.

After the buttery cookies and skim milk, Nana Fanny opens the desk cupboard where she keeps her computer. It sort of rolls out from the wall, very handy. We pull up kitchen chairs and Luna imports the pictures. She has her own file of photos at Nana Fanny's.

"I'll show you the girl," Luna says.

"What girl?" Nana says.

Luna clicks through the photos. "This girl at the Alligator Farm." She comes to a picture of the girl's kitten heels.

"Nice shoes," Nana Fanny says. Like she'd wear them herself if she had half a chance.

Luna says, "There's something wrong with her."

Nana Fanny says, "How do you know?"

I don't want to get involved. A hush comes over us all. I wait to see what Luna will tell her.

"We saw her at the movies before. Remember that?" she says to me.

"There's something creepy going on," I say. Oh, I fall so easily under Luna's sway. "Her name is Bony."

"Bony!" Nana Fanny blurts.

"That's what he called her."

Luna clicks to a photo of the man's shoes. His big toenails are hard gray shells, like something dead. They scare me. I never want to have toenails like that.

"That's her father," I say solemnly, but my voice rises in a question mark.

Another photo unfurls on the computer screen: the man's arm across Bony's chest, whispering in her ear. It was a sneak attack. If you looked from a certain angle, it might just be a dad hugging his daughter. But close-up, you can see that he put his fingers where he shouldn't have.

Nana Fanny rears back and shakes her head. We are so still that we can hear her earrings tinkling. "Oh, girls. I fear for her," she says. "Something's not right. It's not right."

Chapter 2

LUNA

The night we saw Bony and Mr. Creep at the movies, the first time we ever saw them, was a hideous night.

The day started out fab.

First: It was the day before Thanksgiving break.

Second: Bethany Davis snagged me on the way into the cafeteria and asked *me*, the weird, quiet, new girl, if I wanted to hang with her and her friends at lunch.

I abandoned my table of misfits without looking back and thought I had it made, that I'd be in with the Cock-in-a Bay famous and all my troubles would be over and nothing would ever bother me again. Not the fact that Mama was now married to an annoying person named Jimmy, hubby number three. Not the fact that I have a new "sister" who should be starring in a sitcom called "My Animal Friends," whose Facebook cover photo is of two wiener dogs cuddling. Not the fact that I had to leave Tallahassee, the place I lived for seven years, the longest I ever lived anywhere, because Jimbo inherited a crumbling old monstrosity of a B&B and he and Mama suddenly decided that their actual dream in life was to run one. Too depressing.

But with cool new friends, I thought, maybe none of the rest of my sucky life will matter.

Back in Tallahassee, at my old school, the cafeteria has high ceilings and tall windows and stinks like pickle juice, but at Cock-in-a Bay, everything is modern and the smell of Lysol, which is evidently used to keep the white tile floors way too spotless, overwhelms every other smell. There's a constant roar of people yakking and laughing, even though lots of kids don't eat in there. The band geeks cluster on the bus ramp, pretend hippies play hacky-sack and juggle on the back lawn. Juniors and seniors go off campus.

The popular sophomore girls staked out their own table at the back of the room. The tables are small, the size of picnic tables, with fake wood tops. I scooched in on the very end, not daring to open my lunch bag to reveal my hand-packed-by-Mama tomato and mayo sandwich, which I actually happen to love but don't want any of them to know, especially cause there wasn't much food on Bethany's table. Back when Mama had the Sweet Tooth Bakery she put cupcakes in my lunch—usually my favorite, Red Velvet Elvis. But she hasn't baked a single cupcake since we moved.

Bethany, with her round blank face, sat across from me, crunching sweet potato chips. She and her pals wore those thin, blousy tops with chevron stripes or flowers and big plastic statement necklaces. I'm a jeans, t-shirt, and sneakers girl. Would they expect me to start dressing that way, too? Ain't gonna happen.

Bethany untwisted the top of her Hello Kitty thermos bottle, painted metal bangles clinking down her arm. She poured out vinegary-smelling red liquid into the cup and slid it across the table to me.

I asked her what it was.

"Merlot. Red wine. Duh."

I felt my whole self turn red. There was no way in hell I was going to drink red wine in the school cafeteria. "Umm, I'm allergic to red wine," I said, and pushed the cup back to her.

Bethany drank some, then she poured more for her girls. Could I get in trouble for just sitting at a table where wine was being served? The elf-like cheerleading coach was in the front of the room, talking to a fat secretary with no neck. Mr. Fulton and the assistant principal patrolled the perimeter. It was typed in bold in the student handbook: *Automatic six-week suspension for drinking alcohol on school grounds.* So sue me. I didn't want to be kicked out of school and grounded for a year.

Bethany patted her lips. Then she fixed me with her big chocolate drop eyes. "How would you know if you're allergic?"

"Yeah," said her friend Holly, who resembles a heavily-made-up fourth grader. She was chawing on carrot sticks. "Have you drank it before?"

"Drank a whole bottle once. Broke out in hives."

"That's intense," Bethany said, and I thought I was off the hook. But then she said, "Just a sip or two won't hurt you."

"Oh, I *love* Pinot Grigio," said Lindy Mazur. "That's white. If you're allergic to red we'll bring that next time." Ms. Cleavage— the one everyone says has already had a boob job—set them off talking about different kinds of booze that they LOVE and I didn't tell them but I have never had any booze and never will due to Taylor, my real father, being an alcoholic and a pothead.

"Do you bring wine every day?" I asked Bethany.

"Only on special occasions," she said. "Like eating lunch with you, girlfriend!"

"O…kay?" I said, and made a face like, that's weird. Had she been planning to ask me to eat lunch? But inside I was happy. I reached for the cup and—what was I thinking?—I chugged it. It was like sour grape juice.

"YOLO!" said Holly.

"God, I hate that expression," Lindy said. Then she explained to me, even though I hadn't asked, that she was always on a diet and dreamed of mashed potatoes nearly every night. She must weigh all of one hundred pounds. I was dying to dig into my sandwich, but restrained myself.

Then they started in about getting their drivers' licenses—we all have our permits except Lindy Boob-job Mazur, who said she prefers to be driven. Bethany claimed that her grandma is going to get her a new Jeep when she turns sixteen. I didn't say anything about driving—I haven't done much of it, although I've had my permit since May. Mama claims she doesn't have the stomach to teach me.

Bethany bragged about how three guys were begging to go out with her.

Holly Eye-Liner turned to me. "I heard you got hit on by Miller and Coop. They pounce on every new girl. Every halfway-decent new girl."

"Gee, thanks," I said, then I added, the wine talking, "They're both pigs."

All three girls sniggered and nodded, and I wondered what else they'd heard about me.

Coop, in his hipster glasses and pegged jeans, revealed his piggish nature as soon as we were alone in the library at the Sha-Na-Na. Without even a preliminary kiss, and with the door cracked open, he thrust his hand right up my shorts—hello! I still feel sick about the fact that I let him. Let him finger me until *he* got tired of it, even though it felt like being mauled by a large mechanical spider. And then, worse than that, horrible horrible horrible, can't think about it, I shut the door, locked it, and gave him a quick, very quick, blowjob. He ran out afterwards like hellhounds were on his trail and probably blabbed about my easiness all over school.

But Miller, with his longish dark, swingy hair, his shy smile— he hadn't seemed piggish at first. He came over after supper and we played gin rummy and kissed a few times, nice kisses. But then, the next day at school, just like Coop, he ignored me. I'd already crossed him off my daydream list.

The guy I really like, TJ, I'll never tell Bethany about in a million years. Unless we keep drinking together.

The bell rang, and Bethany asked me to meet them at the movie theatre that night for the seven-thirty show of *Did You Hear About the Morgans?* with Hugh Grant and that *Sex in the City* chick. Lindy whispered, "I'll bring the Pinot Grigio." I would've much rather seen *Avatar*, but I said sure.

Mr. Fulton did one more lap around the cafeteria. He's my photography teacher, my favorite. And I had the idea that he might think I'm sketchy for sitting with those girls. Am I sketchy?

Mama and Jimmy *insisted* that I take Nick with me to the movie, because they were going on a "date" to the fancy Cuban restaurant downtown. Cut the act, I wanted to tell them. Skip over the lovey-dovey shit and move on to the divorce already. But I yelled, "Fine!" and hooked on the compass necklace that my best friend back in Tallahassee, Renda, gave me as a going away present. My version of a statement necklace. I'd lusted after that necklace so Renda shoplifted it from The Silver Spider, because that's what true friends do. I was thinking that if I actually did get to be friends with Bethany, Renda might meet her when she came to visit me during spring break. Would they like each other? Somehow I couldn't see it.

Nick barged into my room. "Can I wear your Babar t-shirt?" she said, holding it up in front of her and posing until I finally said yes to shut her up. I wear Babar ironically, but she doesn't.

At the movie theater Nick and I waited for Bethany and company in the musty lobby as long as we could and finally went in to sit down during the previews. I turned around every few seconds to check the door. Bethany didn't come and didn't come and the previews ended and then the movie started and she still didn't come.

"Where's your friend at?" Nick whispered to me, and her

breath smelled like the licorice she was chewing on. Nick wears her hair in a long bob with bangs that hang down in her eyes. She has the most disgustingly perfect hair. "Why not text her?" she asked.

"Don't have her number."

"Doesn't she have yours?"

Why hadn't Bethany asked me for my number? I pretended to be intensely interested in the opening credits. When it finally sank into my thick skull that Bethany really wasn't coming, and had probably never had any intention of coming, I got sick to my stomach thinking about how gullible I'd been. Imagining that Bethany would actually want to be friends with someone like me. Someone who blushes like an idiot and can't form a coherent sentence. Someone who gets zits as big as nipples. Someone who pretends to be allergic to red wine and then chugs it. Someone who gives random blowjobs.

For a few minutes I really thought I might puke. Why did Nick have to be there to witness my humiliation? She'd make fun of me forever. If Nick had been stood up, I would've teased her about it. But when she didn't say anything else, just got caught up in the movie, and when I realized that since school was out for Thanksgiving and I wouldn't have to see Bitch Bethany and her minions for five days, I started to relax.

That's when I noticed the couple we later named Bony and Mr. Creep sitting two rows in front of us. I noticed them because she looked so small and he had his arm around her, not like a father would do, or like I imagined a father would do—slinging his arm over the back of her chair. No, his arm was around her shoulders like she was his date. Bony kept wriggling, but he would just grip her harder. Finally she gave up and sat still.

He leaned over and licked her cheek.

Oh my God. Really?

I elbowed Nick and pointed to them and she nodded and made a yuck-face. The man's silver ponytail hung down over the back of his seat. I could've grabbed it and yanked. Hard. I wish now that I would've yanked it, or kicked him, done something to help Bony.

At school that next Monday I kept my head down in the halls, ear buds in, Arctic Monkeys wailing, dreading my confrontation with Bitch Bethany, until finally, in French class, I overheard two girls gossiping about how Bethany had been pulled out of school. Her parents had taken her on a trip—an *educational trip*. They rolled their eyes. Yeah, sure. The teachers, supposedly, had piled her up with homework. The trip was a big brag all over her FB page. Sickening, the girls complained, and I silently agreed.

Bethany didn't return until a few days before Christmas break. I spotted her at a distance, wearing some batiked blouse from Indonesia, but I came up with an avoidance strategy. I asked Mr. Fulton if I could eat lunch in his classroom and help him catalogue slides. Rack up some volunteer hours for a Bright Futures scholarship. Kill two birds, etc.

When we moved to Coquina Bay I refused to audition for the band because I'd been first chair of the flute section at Raa Middle School in Tallahassee and I was afraid of being demoted, so the only fun class I have now is Fulton's photography class. Fulton is oldish and ex-military and sort of gooney. He's my new favorite teacher.

Fulton helped me get through until Christmas break.

December 23, first day of Christmas break. An important day—we see Bony and Creep again. We didn't have a Christmas tree yet, and all our Christmas decorations, the ones Mama and I collected over the years, were still in boxes somewhere. Mama said they are too busy to think about Christmas just yet, because they want to get the Sha-Na-Na open again right after New Year's, which I'm afraid means that we won't be celebrating Christmas at all. Nick and I both asked for iPhones and have our fingers crossed.

That morning I really got into my photography project. Like, obsessed. And that was my excuse for not helping out around the Sha. Fulton's assignment over the Christmas break was to compile a digital photo album called *How I Survived Being Away From Mr. Fulton for Three Whole Weeks*. It means we can make it be about anything we want. I am planning to be a photographer. I tell adults that I want to be a photojournalist like Dorothea Lange, but really I want to take pictures of haunting people and odd places, more like Diane Arbus's stuff, or like the street people on my favorite Facebook page, *Humans of New York*. In other words, I want to document weird people and shit. Right now I've only got my phone and a Canon Sure Shot, but I need a Nikon, a really good one. That'll have to wait until I win the lottery.

I decided at first to do something practical for my Christmas project—an album depicting the renovation of the Sha-Na-Na. Obvious, right? I took tons of pictures of Mama and Jimmy and the construction crew—including TJ, my crush, a senior at the county high school who has the most appealing arms and hair and ass I've ever seen—sanding, sawing, and hammering, putting in two new bathrooms on the third floor and shoring up the banisters. But pretty soon Mama and Jimmy started asking me to bring them hammers and paint cans and next thing they'd order me to start painting and stop gawking. Plus TJ never even glanced my way, so I gave up on Plan A.

Plan B: I took pictures of the odd things already in the house, like close-ups of the old black and white photographs of strangers in the upstairs hall—relatives of Jimmy's because this used to be his brother's B&B before he died of a blood clot in his brain.

In one of the pictures a dark haired little girl with a silly angelic look on her face perches primly on a cushion. I told Nick that the angel girl was her twin, which made her huff off down the hall.

I snapped some artsy pics of the dumbwaiter. The dumbwaiter is the funkiest thing about the house because it's in a little oily smelling closet and you have to pull it up and let it down by hand. Like the one in *Harriet the Spy*. People who stay at Sha-Na-Na will put their luggage in on the first floor and one of us will pull it up to the second. I could hide inside it, like Harriet did, and watch TJ without him knowing. If I get desperate enough.

I got shots of the big fat banisters carved like grapes. And the stained glass windows with palm trees in the library. By then I'd started admitting it to myself—this is a much cooler house, with more character, than the cottage Mama and I used to live in.

Nick kept hanging around while I took house pictures, trying to get into them, asking to see them, and I missed, with all my heart, being an only child. Even though, over the years, Mama and I have had to endure other peoples' kids in our homes—hippie kids in the New Buffalo commune, and in Taos, our roommate's son Mondo who wore no pants and peed anywhere he felt like it, and in Tallahassee, my stepfather Brad's teenaged devils who descended on us every other weekend—I'd never been forced to live full-time with another kid. It was a dangerous situation. I knew that if Nick kept dogging me I'd have to brain her.

So, Plan C—the Alligator Farm! I got some good shots of the gators and the egrets and the turtles, but I got bored with that. Gators don't do much but lie around, after all. I started taking random shots of the tourists, and it was then I got those good ones of Bony and Mr. Creep. Nick and I talked to Nana about Bony, and Nana agreed that there was something sketchy going on, and I couldn't stop thinking about it.

So tonight when we are all sitting in the mostly empty dining room at the new/old table eating Chinese takeout on the B&B's flowered china plates, I decide to tell Mama and Jimmy about Bony and her inappropriate escort.

Mama and Hubby Number Three are paint speckled and dusty and slumped, exhausted, over their plates of Szechuan Chicken. Probably not the best time to bring up the subject, but I feel compelled to do it. It's my self appointed duty. I rarely miss an opportunity to point out to Mama that many people in our midst are perverted and evil. Just saying. Otherwise she'll go on living in La La Land where everyone is good—deep down—and we all just need to embrace peace and have the right attitude and the Universe will reward us. Oh, yeah, and her third marriage will last forever. Bullshit. She listens to the news. She reads the paper. Her own life, all her previous experiences with flaky men, should prove her theories wrong. But she's eager to keep blocking out all the dark stuff, white-washing the past by explaining that "it was all just a way to the right way." But unless she opens her eyes, like I try to make her do, she'll just keep getting screwed, and I'll have to pick up the pieces.

I stick my snout down in the steamy rice and soy sauce smell and take some deep sniffs to fortify myself. Then I tell Mama and Jimmy about our two sightings of Bony—at the movies and then the Alligator Farm, and Nick puts her two cents in about how Bony looks like a twenty-five-year-old hooker.

Good description. I'm surprised Nick came up with it.

"That creep was holding on to her so she couldn't get away," I say, "like he was her pimp. It was beyond vile."

Mama listens and nods and then says, "That doesn't mean they're not just an ordinary father and daughter. Maybe he's just trying too hard." I *knew* she'd say something like that, bless her heart. Pale green paint dots Mama's cheeks, covering some of her real freckles. She looks like an alien. But she's my alien. Not Nick's. Not Jimmy's. Mine.

Jimmy's got his Tampa Bay Rays cap twisted backwards like a middle-schooler. He says, "Or he might be a stepdad who doesn't know how to relate to his stepdaughter." He points his chopsticks at me. Why does he always think he's funny when he isn't? He's been threatening to join up with those wanna-be pirates who sing in the taverns for tourists. I hope to God he's joking. That's all we need.

But really, TBH, since they got married some things have been better. Jimmy, bless *his* heart, pooh-poohs overpriced organic food and cure-all diet supplements. I no longer have to swallow the ever-changing assortment of horse pills that Mama says will cure all our problems, both mental and physical. Also, unlike Mama's earlier loverboys, Jimmy doesn't drink much or do drugs or have any ex-wives or believe he's a shaman or he can read auras or Tarot cards or is reincarnated from Thomas Jefferson. And the cherry on top—he has a super-sweet mother, Nana, who treats me like her own granddaughter.

He does have flaws, of course, like being a piss-poor driving instructor, having a bratty daughter, and letting Mama do all the parenting. I try to focus on these flaws so that I won't get attached to having him around. That way, when things do fall apart, like they always do, I'll be able to pack my stuff and say *sayonara* without a single tear shed.

Back to Bony and Mr. Creep. "So what if he *is* her father?" I say. "Or her stepfather? It's okay for a father to dress his daughter up like that? And, like, grab her boob?"

"Of course not," Mama says, frowning, her chopsticks pausing halfway to her mouth. "Maybe he did it by accident." She wants me to change the subject. Talking about bad fathers really makes her nervous, because my real father is a doozy.

Wind rattles the old windows in the dining room, and cold air seeps in around the edges. There are no curtains yet. Anyone could be out there in the dark, peering in.

"But he's *not* her father," Nick says. She's actually stopped eating her vegetarian egg roll. "You can tell, if you see them together. She doesn't belong to him." Which is a good way to describe it.

I ordered the Curry Shrimp just to be different, and it's too spicy, but I keep eating it anyway. "He's really mean to her," I add, my sinuses burning. I sniffle. "He was, like, threatening her, telling her he'd feed her to the alligators."

"Well," Jimmy says, "unfortunately, some fathers are mean."

"And clueless," Mama adds, and I know who she means.

I slurp down some ice water, but it doesn't help. "We think he abducted her," I say.

"Nana said she's scared for Bony," Nick adds.

Mama sighs. Any mention of Nana makes her sigh and act put upon. "That woman's always got to stir things up," Mama says. "Everything's got to be a *big* drama. She means well, but…"

"At least she takes us seriously," I say.

Jimbo, scooting rice into a neat pile on his plate with an insistent chop-chop-chop noise, says to Mama, "What about the tile, Darlin'? Mexican or Italian?"

"I'll check it out tomorrow," Mama tells him. More house stuff.

"Don't you think we should do something to help her?" Nick asks.

Jimbo and Mama look at her like they've already forgotten what we were talking about. Mama says that they are probably tourists and that we have to remember that Coquina Bay is much more touristy than Tallahassee, and that the two of them are most likely long gone, and even if there is something fishy going on, how could we prove it? And Jimbo adds that there's nothing we can do anyway, that we don't have enough *evidence* to call the police. That what we'd just told them didn't amount to *evidence*.

"Ev-i-dence," I repeat in a bratty voice.

"This is what happens," Mama tells me in a patient, long-suffering voice, "when you watch those ugly crime shows. And read those gory mysteries. Everybody looks guilty."

"Everyone *is* guilty, Stupes," I say. Mama hates it when I call people Stupes. But now she just sits there smiling her beatific little smile, refusing to take the bait.

"Want some of my mango tea?" Jimmy asks me, holding out his cup, knowing how much I love mangoes.

"No thanks. I don't want your germs," I say, not realizing until I see Jimmy's sad face and Mama's angry face how harsh I sounded.

"That man licked her cheek," Nick puts in. "That is so not right." She won't give up, which I have to admire. In my mind, that's the creepiest thing of all. I hadn't wanted to say the words aloud.

Mama and Jimmy don't react to Nick's revelation. They are both scowling at me, upset about my germs comment. My eyes burn. "What's wrong with you?" I yell at them. "If he'd been raping her right in front of us you still wouldn't care."

Now they're all staring at me like I'm some kind of freak, like only a freak would say such a mean thing. A freak with a dirty mind. A slut who does awful things with any boy who gives her a second look. I get up and leave the table.

Nick's big bedroom is right next to my little tower bedroom. When we first moved into the B&B, I jokingly suggested that her room might be haunted, and sometimes I move things around in her room just to freak her out, which backfired. Now she wants to hang out in my room all the time, which I let her do when I'm lonely. She'll cozy up with the pink and purple paisley comforter on my little iron bed, the one I've had since I was seven, and I settle down in my beanbag chair. Sometimes I get out my flute and play Stephen Foster songs, old rock or new pop tunes—Nick likes anything by Lady Gaga. Sometimes we watch silly YouTube videos or *SpongeBob* or episodes of an old British TV show called *Are You Being Served?* that we both find hilariously awful. (Nick won't watch crime shows with me—too much of a wimp.) We both enjoy stalking people on Facebook.

Sometimes we talk like friends instead of faux sisters. We list the places we miss in Tallahassee—Lake Ella and Maclay Gardens and Ted's Montana Grill. We discuss our parents' lame wedding ceremony, how Mama's dress kept blowing up and showing her saucy underpants and about how Jimmy read that sappy love poem. We snicker about how silly the two of them look together, Mama tall, dark and skinny like Olive Oyl, Jimmy short and muscled—Popeye minus the pipe—and so on and so on, rehashing the past but hardly ever mentioning the present, and never telling our deep, dark secrets. Not that she has any beyond her candy hoarding.

Lots of times I find myself wishing Nick would go back to her own room, but not tonight.

Tonight, after I storm out of the dining room in the middle of the Chinese takeout dinner, I'm relieved to put down my latest British crime novel, *Into the Woods*, when Nick knocks on my door. After all, she hasn't mentioned Bethany ditching me even once. I let her in and cue up Christmas carols on my iPod—Frank Sinatra and Perry Como. We hang the cheap, glittery Christmas stockings we bought downtown over my non-working fireplace. Then we both stretch out on my bed in our flannel PJs and I tell her that I'd been thinking about what Jimmy said about evidence. I tell her that I've made a decision. I want to make my photo album for school be about Bony and Mr. Creep. I'll go around town looking for them—I just know, somehow, that they aren't tourists—and, when I find them, I'll follow them and take secret photographs of them. I'll call my photo album *The Sad Girl at the Alligator Farm* and it will be unusual and journalistic and Mr. Fulton will love it. I'll also be collecting *evidence* that we can show to the police, if we need to.

"I'll come too," Nick says. "You shouldn't go alone. What if he kidnaps you?"

I snort. "It would be better if he kidnapped both of us?"

Frank is singing "Mistletoe and Holly," about the rolls his mother made when she was able. Like making rolls took tremendous effort. Renda and I used to crack up at that one. Lots of things make Renda and me crack up, on occasion laughing until we pee our pants. It feels weird that I don't know exactly where Renda is at this moment, or what she's doing. I could text her, or post on her Facebook page, but doing these things would only remind me how much I miss her and the fact that I won't see her again until spring break.

Nick, on the other hand, is right up in my business. She says in a tough voice, "He can't kidnap you if I'm there. I wouldn't let him."

"What, would you rub chocolate in his hair?"

"Damn straight."

She can be cute. But she can't stop a grown man from doing something he wants to, and I tell her so.

"It'd be more fun doing it with someone else," she says.

"Yeah," I say. "If I was doing it with a friend instead of you."

She slugs me in the boob.

Like Old Mr. Grace says on *Are You Being Served?*—she's a feisty one.

Chapter 3

NICK

I wake up knowing I don't want to find evidence with Luna. While I was asleep, my intuition said, "Stay out of it!" Just like Dad and Kat. If that girl is kidnapped, where are the posters with her photo? Why aren't her parents making a big deal out of it? A little voice inside me says, "How would Dad react if I were kidnapped?" Would he abandon the B and drive around town day and night, showing my photo to strangers? He better be frantic. No one's doing that for Bony, so far as we know, and I'm putting her away in a little box in my mind. If Luna keeps gnawing on it, I'll just get stubborn.

I want an ordinary Christmas, something I haven't had since my mother was alive. My therapist Louise says that it's fine to say exactly what I want. But Kat tells us at noon on Christmas Eve that we're not going to put up a tree. Dad's too busy. She's too busy. I wonder what Louise would say to that? With a therapist there's always a second part. I can imagine her now. *It's fine to ask for what you want. But don't be attached to getting it.* I miss her. She's on vacation in Miami.

Kat says, "We can go downtown to the Festival of Lights and there's your tree!"

She's trying out a cinnamon roll recipe—homemade, with gooey swirls of sugar and cinnamon. Finally, baking. Tearing apart a roll with her fingertips, Kat says, "Besides, we're going to Nana Fanny's to open presents. All the good stuff's hidden in her closet."

I like the sound of that. My phone vibrates and I open it to a text from Maeve Murphy. She's inviting me for a sleepover two days after Christmas. I text back, "Most def."

"Maeve Murphy," I say out loud, to hear the sounds of her name.

"Shut *up*," Luna says. And then, anticipating No-More-Christmas-Trees-Ever, she says to Kat, "What about next year?"

Kat says, "We'll cross that bridge when we come to it. What about the Frost Fair? Today?"

Luna cuts her eyes at me and says, "Whatever." Like she doesn't really care if we go to the Frost Fair. But we already discussed it. We might meet up with friends or girls who might become our friends. And now I might see Maeve there. Something special was happening to me that had not happened to Luna: I was invited to a sleepover. A rare occurrence. "*The Hills Have Eyes*," Luna says in a spooky voice. Meaning she's scared and excited about her search for photo opportunities and evidence.

Dad pops in the dining room and grabs a roll. He wears a t-shirt that has a fiery pirate skull on it. "Hey—TJ can drop you guys at the Frost Fair. We'll pick you up."

Life doesn't get any better than that for Luna, who has an obvious crush on TJ, son of the guy who helps Dad lay tile and hang drywall and paint. She has a secret photo of TJ's tat: a spider on his forearm. TJ's car—a brown Chevy Nova—is parked at our house every day. One girl who came home with me to study for a test actually said, "So does TJ *live* here?"

"Absolutely not," I said. I want a normal family, nothing I have to explain to friends.

"So we can stay out there all day?" Luna says.

"Hey, it's Christmas Eve," Dad says. "We'll come out later. Kat wants to ice skate. Don't you gals want to ice skate?"

We both say sure. Kat gives him a dirty look and picks up her plate and goes to the kitchen. She trashes the pots and plates. Not breaking anything, just banging around a little to let Dad know she's mad. I hope they have a good fight. The last time they had one Dad took me into Jacksonville for a basketball game. Just me.

"Awe-some," I whisper to Luna, a whisper lost in her declaration: "Evidence!" We want different things and the plan seems all jumbled up and happening too fast. I can't tell her that I've changed my mind.

Kat comes out of the kitchen, frowning. "Jim-*mee*," she says, like a warning.

"Hey," Dad says, in a real sweet voice, "TJ's a good driver."

"It's not the driving I'm worried about," Kat says.

Dad doesn't say anything to Kat. He's good at ignoring things. My mother used to say that the house could burn down around him and he'd keep quiet about it. To us, he says, "TJ's got errands to run for me. Get ready!"

We dash up to our rooms and grab a few essentials and pound back down the stairs. Kat comes out of the kitchen. She says, "Whoa, whoa." We stop in front of her for our final instructions. "Stay together. Don't go anywhere else. Keep your phones on vibrate so that I can reach you." She frowns. "Take care of each other. Be good."

"Yes, ma'am," I say, teasing. Being called *ma'am* makes her feel old.

Some outrageous clanging starts from somewhere in the house. Kat sighs. She says, "Get out of here, you lucky ducks." Then, "Seatbelts!"

Outside, it's cold. Dad says we don't know cold, but it's cold for Florida. About fifty degrees. TJ jerks his head to let us know we have to get in the backseat. We shove his tools over. A level. A leather belt with a hammer. And a white bucket filled with rags. His dog Toker sits in the front beside an American Girl Doll dressed like a roller derby princess. With fake boobs and fishnet stockings. Luna wants that doll in the worst way. She'd probably show it off at lunchtime to Bethany.

TJ's a senior, and I think he's been a senior for a couple years. He looks like a swimmer, all muscle. He doesn't like to get his hair cut, and his hair is always streaked from the sun. Kat says it would cost her two hundred dollars to get that done at the salon.

Toker is jet-black, a mongrel with a white star on his rear end. I dig around in my backpack and find a dog treat, a chunk of fake meat with lint all over it, but still, Toker eats it. The Nova smells like fast food grease. And ciggies. And some boy smell—sweat. Gross, gross. It isn't a car you'd want to spend much time inside, but I can feel Luna melting into the seat with glee. The dog sticks his face out the half-rolled-down window to catch the breeze. I like it when dogs do that. They know how to appreciate the little things in life. TJ has some Led Zeppelin playing on the stereo. We inch across Manatee Bridge, bumper to bumper. The sun is shining and the bridge looks golden in the sunshine, like a castle. I want to say, "The bridge looks like a castle," but I know that would be the wrong thing. Babyish. I want to hang with the older kids—acceptance, Louise would say—and I need to stop myself from saying babyish things. Luna and I stare out our windows. With one finger, she spells out B-O-N-Y on my thigh. I move away from her.

We *are* lucky, but not in the way Kat meant. When TJ pulls into the amphitheater parking lot, Bethany is standing there with two other girls and she sees us get out of the Nova and her face looks all confused: jealous, happy. Luna ignores her and leans into the driver's side to say thanks to TJ. She glances away and scans the crowd for Bethany. To make sure Bethany saw her two inches from TJ's face. Next, TJ calls me to his window. "Pobrecita," he says, teasing. *Poor little one.* I'm fourteen, not five, I want to say—I even know a little Spanish, so I'm not a little kid. He has his elbow out the car. Wind ruffles his hair. He reaches down and lightly pounds the door in time to the music. I see how cool he is. Wonder of wonders, TJ slips me a five-dollar bill and winks. No one knows but us. I understand that he does this because, to him, I *am* a little kid. But I feel special. If I see Maeve, I'll buy us each some Frost Fair treat.

Luna stands on tiptoes, trying to see over the heads of everyone. Grown women are dressed as Santa's elves in green-and-red bathing suits with ruffled skirts. Their pointed ears made of green velvet. Their eyelids smeared with sparkly red eye shadow. I smell doughnuts and cotton candy. A Ferris wheel spins and rocks just inside the gate. Christmas lights flash everywhere. You can smell the ocean. People cram up to buy tickets to get in. TJ peels out of there.

"Where'd she go?" Luna says, meaning Bethany. Luna wears a red tank top.

"Aren't you cold?" I pull up my hoodie. "Let's go in. She'll be inside." But I'm not so sure of that. Kids from the high school seem to be hanging around outside, smoking in tight circles under a big tree. Luna goes back and forth—I can read her face. She probably wishes she could ditch me. Well, I won't be ditched. Kat said to stay together. "Can't we ride the Ferris wheel?" I say, in a little sister voice that makes me sick. I'm not little, and I'm not her sister.

We pay to get in and an elf wearing shoes with turned up toes gives us red wristbands to wear so that we can go in and out. Each band has a bell on it. A jingle bell. Luna sticks hers in her shorts pocket.

In the Ferris wheel line, she acts like she doesn't know me. Wind howls off the ocean, not far away. The guy running the Ferris wheel has an eye that wanders, as if he can give a gander in two directions at once. His grin makes me worry that he might speed the thing up or stop the wheel when we're at the top. We get in and the bar bangs shut across our laps. The Ferris wheel jerks into motion and we sweep up to the top, rocking in a way that makes my stomach feel like it's outside of me. Everything down below gets tiny. The lunatic guy running the wheel *walks away*. We're on our own. I reach out for Luna's hand and she squeezes mine. "Don't be a baby," she says. "It's just a Ferris wheel."

Then, "Look," Luna says, "TJ came back!"

There is the Nova in the sunshine, like a Matchbox car I had when I was small. When Dad thought that I ought to have tow trucks and toy cars to make sure I didn't turn into a girlie-girl. I wonder about those errands TJ is supposed to be running for Dad.

And then, our bucket seat swooping down, down, down, I spy that long, white ponytail giving off a glow. Mr. Creep and Bony are leaving the amphitheater, heading toward the parking lot. I scream, "I see them!"

Luna says, "Me, too. Let's catch up."

When we get off the wheel, Bethany hovers. "I've got goodies," she says to Luna, and she shows us a silver flask engraved with designs like a tattoo.

"Luna," I say—a warning.

"Maybe later," she says to Bethany, and she pushes past her into the crowd and reaches for my hand.

I have to look back. Bethany's face has fallen apart. She is not used to being turned down or pushed past. I am proud of Luna. At that moment, for a nanosecond, I sort of wish she were my real sister.

I remind her: "Kat said not to go anywhere else."

Luna says, "Well, are we always gonna do what she says?"

"Uh, *yeah*."

"Speak for yourself. I want evidence."

I stand still and jerk away.

"What?" she says.

"I want to stay here."

"Nickly-Pickly." One of her goofy nicknames for me.

I fold my arms.

"You want something of mine? I'll give you that t-shirt."

I know the one she means: it's more than a t-shirt. It has tiny seed pearls sewn around the scoop neck. And that's how stupid, how easy, I am: I fall for a bribe.

Together we run through the gates, Christmas music blasting. It's like I'm in a movie, running with Luna to "Rockin' Around the Christmas Tree." TJ is still there, the Nova parked beside a clump of boys. They smoke and horse around, jabbing each other and cackling. They sound scary, like they're different when they're clumped together. As if they could hurt me.

We lunge up to TJ's open window.

"What's up?" he says, like he really wants to know.

Luna says, "We have to stand on your car for a second."

"Be my guest," he says.

We jump up onto the hood. I like the view from up there. Everything—Ferris wheel, elves, skating rink, and the steely gray ocean—seems within reach. And there *they* are: Bony being tucked into the passenger side of a red pickup truck and Mr. Creep twirling his keys in one hand and glancing around. He is suspicious of everyone, I believe. His sunglasses give him the look of a long skinny bug with big eyes.

We slither off the hood and Luna tells TJ, "We have to follow that red pickup."

He tosses his cigarette out and says, "Well, get in, girls."

I get in the front seat with Toker, and he wiggles with joy. I squeeze the American Girl doll over a little and strap myself in. Her boobs are made of pieces of Styrofoam egg carton. Covered in duct tape to look like a silver bra. "Go," Luna says, and TJ takes off, gravel flying.

"Not too close," I say.

"Who are those guys?"

"The girl's a girl we know," I improvise. Even though I didn't want evidence—not at all—I liked the way the lie rolls out of my mouth so smoothly.

"We need to know," Luna says, "where he's taking her."

They go through a yellow light and we have to stop at a red. "Shit," I say. But inside, I'm relieved. Can we please go back now? I want to see Maeve. I want a funnel cake.

TJ says, "Bet your mama would not approve of that language."

"Duh." I don't bother to say she's not my mama. I get tired of telling people that.

The red pickup crosses over into a subdivision. When we get through the stoplight, it's easy. Piece of cake, as Dad would say. There aren't many red pickups. TJ says, "You want his license number?"

"That would be good," Luna says. We creep along, not too close. All of the houses look alike, little Florida boxes on the wrong side of the road for the ocean. The people there have to cross the road to get to the beach. The red pickup makes two left turns and TJ follows.

"Looks out of state," he says. "But I can't read it."

Real quick, I open my cell phone and stick it out the window and click the camera.

Luna hauls my arm back inside. "Stay in, you idiot!"

"Don't call me names!"

"He's gonna know we're following him," TJ says.

And suddenly the pickup stops in the middle of the road. TJ slides around him like a snake, as if we're looking for an address. Then Mr. Creep rotates like a robot and stares at us from behind those big black sunglasses. Maybe someone who didn't know us might believe that Luna and I are TJ's sisters. The Nova takes the lead and turns down a narrow street and we stop. It's like we're in the woods with tall pine trees all around. TJ says, "Did you see that rifle in the back window?"

"I did," I say. I am surprised that TJ sounds nervous.

Luna says, "He might be a hunter." She kneels on the backseat, craning to see what she can see.

"Hunter of what?" I say. And I remember the raw, dead nutria they feed the alligators. I feel Toker's dog heart beating. What are we doing on an empty back road with TJ? There is no one around, not a single soul, not a lady gardening, not even another dog. It's so quiet, I hear the palm leaves sawing away in the wind, like eerie music. It's like all the people who live here have gone away for the holiday. Everyone but Bony and Mr. Creep. And I remember my determination not to get involved. Where did it go? Where's my backbone?

"What's this all about?" TJ says. He lights another cigarette. I want to say something smart-alecky to him about smoking, but under the circumstances, it doesn't seem fair. He *is* helping us.

Like an electric shock, my phone vibrates. It's Kat. "Where are you?" she says.

"We just got off the Ferris wheel," I lie.

Chapter 4

LUNA

My stepsister, sharing the passenger seat with a farting dog and an obscene doll, totally clueless as to how lucky she is to be there, proves to be quite a good liar, at least on the phone.

I watch out the Nova's mud-spattered back window for the red truck and I hear her tell my mama, in her sweet little voice, how much fun we are having at the Frost Fair and yes, we'd seen lots of friends from school and yes, we are being careful, and we will wait to ice skate until they get there.

TJ opens the front windows and that makes it way colder in the car. I wish I'd dressed in something warmer than a tank top, but TJ *has* to notice me. I'm also wearing my polka-dotted push-up bra and black thong underwear, which makes me feel sexy even if nobody can see it. If Nick weren't here I'd let TJ see everything in a heartbeat. I conjure up Bethany's face when she saw me with TJ. Priceless.

No sign of Mr. Creep's truck. I slide back down in the seat and face front again. "Let's wait for them to drive by," I tell TJ, just to be talking to him.

"What do you think we're doing?"

I giggle stupidly. "What's your doll's name?"

"Crabatha."

"Ha. If you ever get tired of her, give her to me. Renda would love her. That's my best friend from Tallahassee."

"Shhh," Nick says, like anyone can hear us. Now she's the one turned all the way around, kneeling in her seat, staring over my head. "Where *are* they?" she says. "What are they waiting for?"

TJ and I ignore her. Cold fishy wind blows through the car. Toker sticks his head out the passenger window and sniffs furiously. I'm afraid to turn back around, afraid of what I'll see. Mr. Creep's face. Those sunglasses. That gun in the back window.

"Can I have a smoke?" I ask TJ, not caring what Nick thinks, wanting TJ to notice me *that way*. I've smoked before, but it's not a habit.

"No way. I need my job," TJ says, not looking at me.

Nick gives me a disgusted, knowing look, like she's not surprised I'd smoke. She probably wouldn't be surprised, either, that I'd already had sex, and by that I mean full-fledged fucking, by the time I was her age. I wouldn't recommend doing it the way I did the first time, in a parked Camry with guy who already had a girlfriend, but at least I can check losing my virginity off my to-do list.

"Turn around, baby," I tell Nick, but she doesn't.

TJ stows his cigarette in the ashtray, digs his cell phone out of his jacket pocket and checks it like it's any other day, like he doesn't have a willing hyped-up girl in his backseat, like the three of us aren't hiding from a suspicious creep who noticed that we're following him. Okay, I need to get a grip. First of all, TJ doesn't give a shit about me. Willing or not. And second, Mr. Creep can't know for sure we were following him. Third, since when is it against the law to drive down a public street and then park and just sit there?

It's a pathetic little street. Most of the houses, probably rental houses, look empty. Only two have Christmas decorations in the yards. A brick bungalow has a homemade Snoopy and Charlie Brown, and the other house, what Mama calls an imitation Spanish hacienda, has three light-up reindeer—not lit up because it's still afternoon—the kind that raise and lower their heads like they're grazing. Nothing special, but better than what we have at the Sha-Blah-Blah, which is nothing. Last year, in Tallahassee, Mama and I bought pink lights for the holly bushes.

TJ takes another drag of his cigarette and tosses it out the window. I expect Nick to say something about littering, but she's too busy watching out the back window, which I should've been doing instead of fixating on TJ.

"I got crap to do," TJ says. "Crap I'm being paid to do." His eyes flicker up to meet mine in the rearview mirror, sending me mysterious signals. Or maybe I just want him to be sending me signals. His streaked hair brushes the collar of his frayed jean jacket and I want to touch that hair. I want to touch more than his hair. I want to fling myself on him. Can't he tell? Doesn't he like me at all?

He guns the engine, just slightly. "Back to the Frost Fair?"

"No," I say.

"Yes," Nick says at the same time. She gives me a panicked look. "There he is," she says in a squeaky voice.

I swivel around.

The pickup rolls behind us like a shiny red fish gliding through water. I lift my camera and snap some quick shots of it through the back window. The truck rumbles past, Mr. Creep and Bony both looking straight ahead. It keeps going down the block and then swerves up into the driveway of a peach-colored stucco house and disappears around back.

"Come on," I say to TJ. "Let's drive past their house real slow. I need more pictures." Can't believe I'm bossing him around. Bethany would be so jealous.

"Okay, Nancy Drews. What the hell's going on?"

Nick sinks down, still facing me. "We don't know," she says.

"We don't know what's going on. She wants to find out. I don't."

"The pictures are for a project," I say, "for school. It's called *Pickup Trucks and the Men That Drive Them.*"

Nick gives a little snort of laughter and then covers her mouth. "Bullshit."

"I'm going to be a photographer," I add.

"So?" There's a buzzing noise in the front seat. This time it's TJ's phone. "Hold on," he tells us. He pulls his cell out of his jacket pocket again and checks the screen. He must not like what he sees on the screen, because he shakes his head and starts texting someone.

I know he has a girlfriend. A senior. A varsity cheerleader with long bouncy black hair.

There's a swooshing sound when he sends the text. He says, "We're not moving until you tell me the real reason."

Nick shrugs at me and I go ahead and tell him the truth, tell him what we think about Bony and Mr. Creep, about Project Sad Girl and my quest for evidence.

"It's really none of our business," Nick says. "That's what I think."

"Shut up, Lardy Lady," I tell her.

She makes a nasty face, but TJ seems interested. "You're this close," he says, turning all the way around to look at me. He grins. One of his tan cheeks has a little triangular dimple. "Go up and ring his doorbell. I dare you." He turns the car engine off.

Oh, that dimple. "Okay," I say. I jump out of TJ's car. But then I stand there on a scruffy strip of brown grass, car door still open, staring over at the house.

"Wait a minute," Nick says, not moving from the front seat. "What about the gun?"

"Ah," TJ waves his hand dismissively. "It's just a hunting rifle."

"What are we going to say when they come to the door?" Nick asks me.

"Just ding-dong-ditch 'em," TJ says, and snickers. He's not taking this seriously.

"Come on," I say. "TJ, come with us."

"I got some business to transact right here," TJ says. "Ya'll go ahead."

That's why he wants us out of the car. I hope he's not up to something illegal. He named his dog Toker, which isn't a good sign. Maybe he's under police surveillance right now. He could be just as dangerous as Mr. Creep, but I doubt it. I sure don't want him to be.

Nick still looks undecided. She scratches Toker's head and he licks her wrist.

"We'll take Toker," I say, knowing that if Toker comes, Nick will come, too. And TJ won't drive off and leave Toker. "Got a leash?" I ask TJ.

"Never use one. He'll stick right with you," TJ says. "Go on, boy."

Toker jumps out and sits right down on the sidewalk beside me.

Nick finally climbs out of the front seat, hugging herself. She yanks up the hood of her jacket. "This is really stupid," she says. "It's all your fault if something bad happens."

It is stupid, but I'm used to doing stupid things. Maybe not this stupid. My heart speeds up. "If we get enough evidence we can go to the police and maybe save the girl and be interviewed on *Dateline*," I tell her. "Wouldn't that be cool? Shouldn't we try?"

"I guess," Nick says.

"We need a plan."

She crouches down to kiss Toker's snout. "We could pretend to be selling something." Toker licks her chin. "But we don't have anything."

"Or, we could say that we found this dog and we're wanting to know where he lives."

"What if Mr. Creep says Toker *is* his?"

"Then we'll run away. With Toker."

On the way to Bony's house Nick and I discuss whether or not we should ring some other doorbells just to make our lie more believable, but decide that we don't want to waste time, so we keep walking. Toker, oblivious as to the reason for our walk, trots between us.

I'm shivering and my bare arms have goose bumps. My thoughts skitter all over the place. Where is our Florida sunshine? High school band music from the Frost Fair, across the highway and beyond the woods, fades in and out. It sounds so wholesome. I miss being part of a big sound. I miss my nerdy band friends. What am I doing here? TJ's dimple is delectable. It has to be late afternoon by now. I left my cell phone in the car. I don't want Mama worried about us. Did she believe Nick's lies on the phone? If not, we'll never hear the end of it.

There's a little wooden sign out front of Bony's house that says, "Happy Hideaway." Maybe it's a hideaway, but no way is it happy. It's a bland stucco house with nothing inviting about it.

I peer around the side. The red pickup is parked in back, sideways, so I can't see the license, but I take quick pictures of the truck and the house without looking at the camera screen.

"What if he sees you taking pictures?" Nick asks me, the hood dwarfing her face.

"He won't. Don't worry." I sound like a big sister. I've never been a big sister. Being a big sister means that everybody will blame me, not her, if something bad happens.

Nick looks terrified, and I feel jittery myself, like that cartoon roadrunner ready to spook. Mr. Creep is bad news, and Nick and I are about to waltz right up and knock on his door. If this was a horror movie, the audience would be yelling at us right now, telling us to run as fast as we can back to TJ and his stinky car. But still. Like TJ said, we've come this far. And that evil man should not be allowed to get away with this. "It's for Bony," I tell Nick. "We gotta do it."

Nick shakes off the hood, straightens her shoulders, like someone about to make a sales pitch, steps up onto the stoop and rings the doorbell. The donging echoes inside the house. Nothing. Toker sniffs around an empty clay flowerpot on the porch. Nick rings the bell again. I climb up beside Nick and Toker.

The door creaks open and Bony stands there. It's hard to tell exactly how old she is. Her outfit is straight out of *Real Housewives*. She's wearing a cropped hoody and matching sweatpants, hot pink, the expensive, velvety kind, so new they have creases in the legs and sleeves. But her dull brown hair hasn't been brushed in awhile. She glances from me to Nick to Toker with no expression on her pale face. She doesn't look scared, relieved, sad, pleased, nothing. The cute, superior, flirty attitude is history. She doesn't say a word.

For a second I can't remember what we planned to say. "We were wondering," I finally blurt out, "is this your dog?"

"We found him just down the street," Nick adds. "He's such a nice dog we knew he belonged to somebody. I'd love to keep him but, you know, if he's yours…"

Bony glances into the dark hallway behind her. Then she turns back to us and her mouth twitches a little, but she doesn't respond to our question.

I pull my camera out of my jacket pocket and take a picture of her, real quick, not bothering to explain myself. "So, this *isn't* your dog?" I ask, my voice sounding loud and false. "Do you know whose it is?"

From inside the house comes a kid's voice, calling, "Bony?"

There's another kid? In the house with that monster?

Then there's a loud tromping sound. Bony hops outside onto the stoop and shuts the front door behind her. She's barefoot. Without saying a word she grabs hold of my wrist and tugs, like she wants me to go somewhere with her. Is she trying to escape? Should we help her? Can she talk?

Nick and I don't have time to debate, but we're both thinking the same thing. Nick stumbles down the front steps, Toker at her heels. "Can you go to the Frost Fair with us?" she asks Bony. "It's really cool."

"Come on," I say. "We'll go ice skating."

The front door flings open and Mr. Creep stands there, hands on his hips. He wears a Santa hat on the back of his head, cocked at an angle. Very tall and skinny. He says in an angry, but not yelling, voice, "Where the hell you going, girl? Who are you people?"

"We found this dog," I manage to say. I finger the Frost Fair wristband in my pocket and squeeze the smooth little jingle bell.

"Bo-ny!" A woman flies out of the house, pushing past Mr. Creep, a very suntanned woman in a black cami and white shorts. She's a step down from *Real Housewives*. She could be a hostess on one of those shopping channels, a chick that's spent too much time partying. Her skin's leathery and she sports tons of gold jewelry—necklaces, bracelets, and a sparkly ring on every finger. In one hand she grips a plastic glass of something with ice.

"Why weren't you watching her?" Mr. Creep says to the tanned woman. "She's not supposed to answer the door."

The woman smiles at us. She has very white teeth. "Hey, girls," she says. "Don't mind him. We're on vacation with the grandkids. Mason is sooo over protective." Her voice has a boozy slur. "Bony, honey, come on back up here."

Mr. Creep—Mason—has a wife? Why did she feel the need to explain that they were vacationing with the grandkids? TMI. Maybe it's just me, but the three of them don't seem like they go together, not in the regular family way. And why have we only seen Mr. Creep and Bony out places together? Where have the wife and other kid been?

Bony remains planted on the walkway, bent over, patting Toker, more like grabbing handfuls of his fur and squeezing, but he doesn't seem to mind.

"Back inside, Bony," Mr. Creep says. "Now."

Bony acts like she doesn't hear him.

Nick's eyes meet mine and I can tell she doesn't know what to do either. We can't help Bony now. Should we make a run for it? Or take a fast picture of Mr. Creep and then make a run for it? That's what a photojournalist would do.

The drunk woman bustles down the front steps, smelling like coconut lotion and booze, the way my father used to, and swings Bony up into her arms like a toddler.

"Is she okay?" Nick asks the woman. "Can she talk? Is her name really Bony?"

Nobody answers Nick's questions. Mr. Creep, lurking in the doorway, is silent and glowering. Bony hangs stiff in the woman's arms, staring down the street.

TJ's Nova pulls up, music blasting.

I've never been more relieved to see a car in my life.

"Bony's shy," the woman says. "Her baby brother never shuts up. Merry Christmas, ya'll!"

"Merry Christmas," Nick says.

Bony, perched on the woman's hip, glances down at us with a solemn expression, like she wants to say something but doesn't see the point. I pull the Frost Fair wristband out of my pocket and slip it onto her wrist. She shakes her thin little wrist and the bell tinkles. "Merry Christmas," I add.

"Aren't you a sweetheart," the tanned woman says. She doesn't look me in the eyes. Clutching her drink and Bony, she carries them both back up the stairs, Bony's pale foot flopping against the woman's brown thigh, loose, like she's given up. They push past Mr. Creep and into the house.

"Who's that?" Mr. Creep says, nodding his head toward TJ. "Saw that guy earlier."

"My boyfriend," I say at the same time Nick says, "My brother!"

"He was helping us find the dog's owner," I add.

TJ honks the horn like he needs to announce his presence.

Nick and Toker and I run toward the car. When we are safely inside, me in the front seat this time, I glance out the window. Mr. Creep has gone back inside and the house looks vacant again. It's like the whole weird thing never happened.

"Did you get all the clues you need?" TJ asks us as we rattle back toward the Frost Fair.

I turn down his stereo. "It's even more confusing now," I say.

TJ drives while I turn around and Nick and I scroll through my pictures. Mr. Creep's truck ahead of us. Passing us. The stucco house. The red truck in back. Bony, standing in the doorway.

"Were they telling the truth?" Nick asks me.

I can tell by her voice that she doesn't think so, either. I swing back toward TJ and straighten Crabatha in the seat beside me. I leave one of her legs cocked up at a flirty angle.

"Can I please have that doll?" I wheedle. "Can I at least borrow it?"

"Never," TJ says.

Nick says, "How you gonna get back into the Fair without your bracelet?"

I shrug. I hadn't thought of that.

Then TJ gets involved, telling us how there's a gap in the fence around back of the Frost Fair and that Nick can go into the fair first and I'll wait outside by the gap and then Nick will pass her bracelet to me so I can come in without having to pay.

Which is what we end up doing. It's the third thing we've done that day that we could get into big trouble for. But as my dad says, if you break curfew, might as well stay out all night. Maybe I'm more like him than I'd ever admit.

•

Mama and Jimmy are waiting at the ice rink, and they never ask us a thing about where we've been. None of us can skate very well, but we nearly kill ourselves trying, falling down on the soft, puddly "ice" and clambering back up to try again. Thankfully, nobody I know is there to witness the spectacle. Bethany and her minions are gone. TJ and his crowd are gone. It's mostly couples, holding hands, and families, holding hands. It gets dark and it's all about the lights and the Christmas music and the four of us laughing and staggering and falling. The exercise makes me nice and warm.

Then I twist my ankle, just a bit, but I can't skate. Jimmy gives me his leather jacket and I sit on the sidelines in my sock feet, sipping watery hot chocolate, my stinky brown rental skates with their broken and re-tied laces lying in a heap beside me. I snap pictures of my new so-called family when they go teetering past, Mama in her red cardigan, Jimmy in his Christmas scarf, and Nick, hood up, who always remembers to wave at me. Our neighbor Molly and the rodent guy from the Alligator Farm go stumbling around the rink again and again like two drunks having a grand old time.

It *had* been fun, while we were skating, but the longer I sit there, watching the other skaters, the gloomier I get. The Frost Fair. What a joke. All fake. Fake, fake, fake. Why are we pretending this is anything except a semi-tropical climate? Why are the four of us pretending to be a family? We are just as phony as Bony's family.

I think about my dad, Taylor. The last letter I got from him, in October, was from Washington State. He'd bought some land there, he wrote, and was camping out on it. "The farther from here, the better," was Mama's only comment.

One Christmas we went up to visit his parents in New Hampshire, and a bunch of us went cross country skiing in a state park at night, the trail marked with luminarias—candles inside paper bags. I kept falling down then, too, but he'd stayed right with me the whole way.

That was real winter, real snow, a real Christmas. The way it's supposed to be.

This is just pathetic.

Later, before I go to sleep, after I try unsuccessfully to reach Renda on the phone, when Nick is snoring in her own room, I download the Bony pictures onto my laptop, enlarge and study them. It is possible, I know, that Nick and I totally misread the situation. We want to see a mystery where there isn't one. Two bored idiots, looking for excitement, wanting a secret that will bond us together, conjuring up something out of nothing. Actually, Nick wasn't into it as much as I was. I was the one pushing to find evidence. I flush with embarrassment for myself. It could be that Mr. Creep—Mason—and Ms. Suntan and Bony and her brother *are* an actual family. An unhappy family, maybe, a weird family, a mismatched family, a fucked-up family, but so what? There are plenty of those. I've lived in a few of them myself.

As I'm studying the picture of Bony standing in the doorway of the Happy Hideaway, something catches my eye. Right where her sweatpants and cropped sweatshirt come together, there's a dark spot. It might be a birthmark. Or a bruise. Or just a shadow. Something out of nothing. Here I go again.

Her eyes, though. Her eyes mesmerize me. They bore right into me. Like she's trying to tell me that she needs help. Letting me know that I'm the only one who can help her. Or maybe I have just seen too much *Dateline*. Maybe I just want be a hero. With one click, I make her eyes go away.

I download the skating pictures. One of them is pretty good, because of the different expressions on all three of their faces. Mama wide-eyed, open-mouthed but still beautiful, trying to keep her balance. Jimmy, plaid scarf around his neck, chest thrust out, a serious expression, like a figurehead on a ship. Nick in the middle, laughing with her eyes closed, skates just about ready to slide out from under her.

Then I see the man behind them, standing at the side of the rink. He's looking directly at the camera. Directly at me.

Mr. Creep. Wearing his Santa hat. White ponytail curling around his shoulder like a white worm. A maggot.

Chapter 5

NICK

My real mom did special stuff on Christmas morning. She'd set what she called her internal alarm for six in the morning and slip through the house to my room. We lived in a *Florida* house, a ranch house with a screened-in porch and a palm tree in the yard, not a rickety mansion like the B. Light as a whisper, she would raise my covers and get into my bed. Her neck and arms always smelled like J'Nate, a lemon body splash. Her toes would be cold. Like ice cubes. I pretended to be asleep. She sang a silly Christmas song she made up when she was little.

> *When we wake up, stars are twinkling.*
> *Raisins popping out of cross buns.*
> *All the giftwrap will be crinkling.*
> *Christmas morning, da-da-de-dum . . .*

My real mom was a first grade teacher so she could be silly. Professionally silly. Kat would never sing a song that makes her look goofy. She takes everything super-super-seriously and she likes to say, "Everything happens for a reason," and "There's bound to be a karmic lesson here." Dad does all the goofy stuff in their duo.

What I liked best was the way my real mom kissed my forehead until I let her think she was waking me up. We would snuggle there until Dad hollered, "Come and get it!" That meant that the coffee and hot chocolate were ready.

Thinking about her makes my heart hurt. I remember the sleepover only two days away and I concentrate on that, like a secret chocolate bar, something to make me feel better.

Here we are now, six years later in our new life, and I hear Dad out there in the hallway, pulling the cords on the dumbwaiter, bringing up the hot chocolate on a tray. The house is quiet, a little before seven. The cups and saucers clink and tinkle against each other. The door to my balcony is open a crack and a slice of cool air whizzes around the room like a ghost.

Then: big smoky fireworks go off somewhere. Like we're in a war. Dad knocks.

I say, "Come in, Mr. Rat Hair," what I used to call him when I was about three.

He flips on the too-bright chandelier. He sings Mom's silly song. He hasn't put in his contacts yet; his black glasses make him look like Roy Orbison. Except I doubt if Roy Orbison would've been caught dead in a pirate t-shirt. Suddenly I want to sit around with Dad all day and watch rock and roll DVDs. Forget Christmas. But the show must go on. That's what Dad used to say right after Mom died.

He delivers my hot chocolate and then he goes next door to Luna's and delivers hers. He forgets all about the snuggling part. He probably thinks I'm too old for that. I probably am, Louise might say.

Our house is so close to Molly's that I hear her calling her dog, Wooster. Out my window I see her on the side porch, lit up by the porch light, dressed for church in a long velvet skirt and a pink sweater. But it's only seven in the morning, so my imagination goes wild. She must have stayed up all night. With that guy from the Alligator Farm, the one who hauls in the bloody carcasses of nutria. What did they do together? Was it anything like what I do to myself? I shut that picture like a book. I don't want to go there. Her porch is decorated with wreaths and plaid bows. She's like an animated Christmas card you'd find in your email. She waves to me, her fingers dancing like she wants to write something happy on the air. It looks cold out there. Cold and dark.

I sip my hot chocolate. Kat left the spoon on the saucer so that I can spoon up the tiny melted marshmallows. Everything's okay, everything's okay, I tell myself, but I miss my real mom. Louise says I'm having anxiety attacks about it. She says that if I name the feeling, it won't bother me so much. Does Dad miss her, too? We used to talk about it, but after he and Kat got together, we stopped. It was like when the electricity goes out. One day it was fine to talk about it and the next day—ka-boom—I just got the feeling that it wasn't fine anymore.

That overhead light makes everything in my room seem shabby. Dad hasn't painted it yet. Red swirly wallpaper peels from the corners. I wish I were getting a puppy for Christmas, but I've been down that road with Dad and know it's impossible. Sha-Na-Na is almost a public place and we have to be prepared for people—guests—with allergies. They're our bread-and-butter, our college funds. Blah, blah, blah. I wish I had a puppy to snuggle with. Can't we just warn the people with allergies? *Don't Come Here If You Have Allergies To Cute Dogs*. I guess you might say I'm feeling sorry for myself. Then I remember Bony. How's she feeling? Do they have a Christmas tree? Does she miss her real mom? Does Mr. Creep come in and try to snuggle her? A sickening thought.

The doorbell rings. It's a funny old doorbell that sounds like a buzzer on a game show. Someone leans on it hard.

Luna, Dad, and I come together on the landing, everyone

frowning, wondering who would ring our bell so early on Christmas. Luna's outfit is fashion-crazy: Lycra top and skinny pants and a torn shirt and Converse sneakers. Ooh—she's got those skinny legs. I am planning to wear baggy cargo pants. A plain t-shirt.

"What the hell?" Dad says.

"What the hell?" Luna says.

Dad taps her on the back of the head for cursing. If he only knew.

We peer down the steep stairs to the foyer. Kat goes to the front door in her fuzzy robe and flip-flops. The enormous wooden door—from the 1800s—has long windows on either side of it. Kat peeks out one of the side windows and she leaps back—frightened? Or just surprised? She glances over her shoulder at us.

"Who's there?" Dad says, a manly tone in his voice. He might have to protect us.

"It's . . ." Kat presses her hand on her heart. She sends a helpless look all the way up the stairs to Luna. "It's your . . . dad," she croaks.

"Dad?" Luna says, and she sort of floats down the stairs in her new sneaks, like someone who has a date with destiny. All of a sudden, it isn't just Christmas. It's *The Christmas Luna's Dad Came Back*. The Christmas he crashed our Christmas.

Does Kat think this is her karma? Karma being revenge by the universe. Because it certainly isn't mine. She opens the door and there he stands, in a cheesy Santa hat, holding two skateboards decorated with red devils and flames. An earring dangles from one of his earlobes. Luna skids to a stop right beside Kat. Her dad stays on the outside. No one invites him inside. Cold air whooshes in. But he stays right there, hanging onto those skateboards like life preservers.

"Merry Christmas, ladies," he says. He pulls off the Santa hat and nods toward Dad. "You, too, Jimster." Luna's dad's voice is hoarse, like he has a sore throat. His haircut's fresh. You can see his pink scalp.

"Likewise," Dad says.

"Well, come on in," Kat says. She doesn't sound like she means it. It sounds like, "Go away!"

"For a few minutes, maybe," he says. And he steps over the threshold and Kat shuts the door.

I can't see Luna's reaction. But she doesn't rush up to hug him. She stays close to Kat. Kat puts her arm across Luna's shoulder.

"This here skateboard's for you," he says, offering it to Luna. He glances up at me. "And one for you, too, sister."

He rolls one of the skateboards toward the foot of the stairs. I say nothing.

"Thanks," Luna says, like he's giving her a stick of gum. Not much. But she tucks it under her arm. "How'd you know what I wanted?"

Who's she kidding? I think she'd prefer a Camry.

Her dad taps his forehead and grins. "Intuition."

Kat sighs real big. Like she never wants to hear that word again. But, in fact, she *loves* intuition. So long as it's *her* intuition. Dad goes down the stairs and says, "Taylor, you'll have a little breakfast with us, won't you?" They shake hands.

And I'm left at the top of the stairs alone. Left out. Now Luna has two fathers and a mother. They look sort of like a family down there. Whole lotta blending going on, I tell myself in a smart-aleck tone. I go back into my room and taste my hot chocolate. It's cold.

When I finally get dressed and go downstairs, Kat's serving gooey warm cinnamon rolls and hard-boiled eggs. They're all seated at the huge long table, Kat, Dad, and Luna at one end, and Taylor at the other. Taylor smells like cigarette smoke. He and Dad are talking about football. The windows in the dining room are so old that the glass is wavy. I sit down very close to Dad and focus on my face in the wavy glass. I look like someone in a photograph from another century, the century before the last century—yikes!

Almost like the photographs upstairs in the hallway. Like a ghost. I'd put my hair in braids like sprouts. Luna would probably say that I needed a makeover. If she wasn't so busy being the queen bee.

"Look what the cat drug in," Taylor says.

"Taylor," Kat scolds.

"Teasing," Taylor says.

So that's what he's like: a mean guy who teases. He'd probably say he teased me because he *likes me*. I can't stand people like that. "I don't care," I say. "You're more like what the cat *dragged* in."

"Touché," he says.

Dad squeezes my knee and says, "Little Miss Grammar Puss."

Luna doesn't want to be left out, so she says, "How'd you get here, anyway?"

Taylor points to his mouth to let us know he wants to swallow before he answers. His mouth is crammed full of cinnamon roll. He hums, "Mmm, mmm," to let Kat know how good they are. We wait, everyone watching him. He has a blurry tattoo on one hand—a bird with a word coming out of its mouth. I can't tell what word.

Finally he says, "My car's a few blocks away. I ran out of gas."

"Your idea of living on the edge?" Kat says.

Dad rescues Taylor and says, "Lots of places probably closed early."

"You got that right," Taylor says.

"You can ride with us to Nana's. Right, girls?"

Luna and I cut our eyes to each other, but I can't read what she's thinking. Kat pushes away from the table. "Have yourself a merry little Christmas," she says, under her breath. She gets up and goes in the kitchen. Luna goes with her. I busy myself mashing butter and salt into my hard-boiled egg. I mash it up good.

Dad says, "There's only one NFL game today. But there's plenty of basketball. The Heat play the Knicks at noon. Want to watch that? After the presents?"

"Thanks, Jimster," Taylor says. "I don't know if I'm welcome."

"Hey, it's Christmas, " Dad says. "You're welcome."

Taylor sits in the backseat, wedged between Luna and me. The seatbelt in the middle is stuck down inside the seat and he says, "That's okay. Won't be the first time I rode somewhere without a seatbelt."

In the front passenger seat, Kat says, "We don't want to know." She jams her sunglasses on and locks her seatbelt.

Two grocery bags of wrapped presents are in the hatchback. And the skateboards—Taylor wants to see them under the tree. Kat has stashed plenty more presents at Nana Fanny's.

In his hokey pirate voice, Dad says, "The captain of our stout ship and merry band prefers a little rock and roll. And walk the plank if ye don't want it, too." He slips in Lynyrd Skynyrd's Christmas CD. I expect Kat to question whether he's really the captain or not, but she keeps mum. She's not feeling joke-y.

I tuck in my ear buds and listen to my own music, what I'm in the mood for—Avril. Luna does the same. We are off in our own little worlds. Everyone is.

But when we are almost to the turn for Nana Fanny's house, I see a red pickup and I reach across Taylor's back and poke Luna.

"What?" she says, annoyed, ripping out her ear buds.

"Mr. Creep," I mouth.

Taylor says, "No secrets back here."

"Never mind," Kat says.

Luna rolls her eyes. Her scary black eyes. Then Dad turns left and we enter Nana Fanny's Queendom, her neighborhood in which no one stirs, ever. I will be glad to see Haiku.

When we get out of the car, Taylor says, "This is nice." Then: "Oops. Looks like she's got a cop for a neighbor."

"So?" Luna says.

Taylor says, "Just saying."

A policewoman named Sherry lives across the street. Her squeaky-clean cop car is parked in front of her garage. Like maybe she's about to go on duty. I know Sherry, but Luna does not. Once when I slept over at Nana's, Sherry came to visit—in gym shorts and a sports bra—and she and Nana stayed up late, talking about boyfriends and how to get along with them. Or not. I watched a talk show on the little kitchen TV and pretended not to listen. I admired Sherry's muscles. They glistened.

At the door, when Nana Fanny opens up, Dad kisses her cheek and says, "Mom, this is Luna's dad. Taylor. He's having Christmas dinner with us."

"I'm Frances," Nana Fanny says. "Merry Christmas."

That's Nana Fanny. She rolls with the punches. She's probably thinking, "The more, the merrier." Or maybe she misses having two sons.

"Ma'am," Taylor says shyly.

We all go in and Haiku comes barking, barking, barking. He's worried about Taylor. But one thing about Taylor is that he's good with dogs. He talks to them in a voice filled with love and respect. He gets down on one knee and says, "Hey, buddy, let's be friends."

Haiku licks his hand right away. Then he leaps into his arms.

Nana Fanny says, "That just warms my heart."

Kat does not say anything. Her heart does not seem warmable today. She gathers our jackets and goes to the hall closet and carefully hangs up everything. Taking her time. Her sweet time, Dad would've said, if it mattered to him. Luna waits for Kat where the hall begins. Nana Fanny's tree is humongous. It touches the ceiling. It's a real tree and smells like a real tree. Presents are stacked all around, almost color-coordinated. Taylor tucks the skateboards he brought up under the tree. The decks are dinged-up. The wheels are scratched. Like skateboards he found at a garage sale. Or stole.

Haiku is on Taylor's lap. Dad turns on ESPN. Dad and Taylor settle in, but Kat and Luna and I are restless.

Luna spreads all the other presents around, under the tree and on the side tables. She says, "So when do we get the loot?"

Kat says, "That's up to Nana."

In her amazingly red dress with its orange belt trimmed in African trading beads, Nana says, "I'll get drinks all around and then we'll start." She grins, her wattle wattling. She clicks her heels together and that's when I notice her shoes: flats made of leaf-like scraps of leather, pink and red and orange.

"Nice shoes," I say.

Kat says, "I need to make a phone call." Translation: I need to escape. She smiles a fake smile and says, "Think I'll go out on the patio and make a phone call. My sister." Her freckles make a mask on her face like tiny copper beads. That might not sound beautiful, but no doubt, she's beautiful. She slides back the big glass door that leads to the patio.

Nana says, "Girls, you want to help me?"

Luna says, "Think I'll watch TV."

What a relief that Luna doesn't want to hog all of Nana's attention.

I go into the kitchen. It smells so good. Oranges and cinnamon and bacon. Even though I don't eat meat, I still like the smell of bacon. It's homey.

"Time for second-breakfast?" I say.

Nana pulls a tray off the top of the fridge. She puts out a Christmas mug for each person. Then she says to me, in a soft voice, "Do you miss your mom, sweetheart?"

And I burst into tears.

I want to hide. Especially from Luna's dad. He seems like the kind of dad who blurts out things that hurt your feelings.

Nana Fanny takes me in her arms. I cry all over her dress. She doesn't care and that's one reason why I love her. "Come in here," she says, and she tugs me into the walk-in pantry. It smells like chocolate chips and brown sugar in there. She wipes my face with tissue and hugs my shoulders.

I say, "I feel just like I did the day she died." My mother was a jogger and a driver talking on a cell phone slammed into her. At first I thought she was sick in the hospital, but after a day, Dad sat me down and told me she was gone. His face was all swollen up from crying. It hurt so bad to see him crying.

"Just like?" Nana Fanny says.

"Maybe not that bad," I say. "But at Christmas you miss your mom."

"Did you ever open that box?"

"What box?"

"Your mother's things."

I shake my head violently. Like everything in there might rattle loose.

"You feel abandoned?" she says.

I don't like that word. It makes me think about how Dad must have felt when Nana Fanny ran off and left him and his brother in Key West. I shrug away from her. Can I trust her? Or anybody?

She says, "Sometimes a good cry is the best medicine." And: "I miss her, too."

I've turned into a crybaby. Kat says it's my age and that I'll get over it. But one day at school I started crying in the hallway and the janitor saw me and said, "What if your face froze like that?" That seems like the kind of thing Taylor might say and I don't want to give him the chance. I like him for his dog-sense and then I think he doesn't have much girl-sense.

Back in the kitchen I eat two big cookies. Chocolate therapy.

Nana Fanny says, "Do you want to take some cookies over to Maeve?"

"No way." I might burst into tears in front of her and it'd be all over school the first day back.

There's so much to worry about. My weight. My secret eating. My nighttime secret. Dad and Kat's fights. Mom. And now Taylor.

One thing our family does not need is someone else to blend into it.

Then there's Bony. Would Mom want to rescue Bony? I wish she'd speak to me in the night about it. I feel Luna getting me back into it. Last night she said, "Wouldn't you want someone to rescue you if you were her? Ignoring it's an evil thing." If only I'd get a signal from Mom about what to do—I'm waiting for that. If I tell Luna that my real mother doesn't want me to get involved she'll back off, for sure. There's something about Bony I would never tell anyone. I hate how cute she is.

I want to crawl into Nana Fanny's bed and watch TV. She has R-rated movies I can get away with watching. Love stories gone wrong. But no. Dad comes into the kitchen and says, "What'samatter, Princess?" He sits down at the kitchen table and makes me sit on his lap. "None of your beeswax, Mr. Rat Hair," I say. No way will I tell him with Kat nearby. The radio is tuned to Christmas music. He and Nana discuss Christmas—what it was like when Dad was small and they lived in Key West in the hotel that Dad grew up in. Nana Fanny says, "Did I ever show you the poem I wrote about that old guy who came every year?"

"Yes," Dad says. In other words, I don't want to see it again. Then, "The show must go on." He kisses my forehead and pats my back in a way that says, "Time to get up now."

We open presents. I thought that I was over crying, but the whole time we are opening presents, I feel almost like crying again. I want Kat to be in a good mood. I want Taylor to disappear. I want Dad to be extra nice to Nana Fanny. I get the iPhone from Santa. But I *don't* get the Ballasox flats I asked for. Instead it's a cheap pair from Dillard's. And the usual stuff—a necklace, pajamas, a sweatshirt, shower gel, socks, and chocolate bars.

Kat is quiet until she opens the last present, the box from Dad—a pasta maker and a wooden rack to hang the homemade pasta on. "Just what I wanted!" she says. And she leans over and gives Dad a big smooch on the cheek. Taylor stares out the window, his mouth sagging. I think it must make him sad to see Dad getting the love he used to get. Dad seems embarrassed—does he feel selfish for marrying Kat?

Then everyone looks at the ceiling or the muted TV. It feels like being locked in a teeny-tiny closet with all of them. Locked in but trying not to touch each other. Claustrophobic.

Taylor says, "So—blimey, me gals—let's have a skateboard lesson."

He's trying to imitate Dad's pirate talk, but I don't care. I just thank my lucky stars he gets us out of there.

Chapter 6

LUNA

When Dad showed up on Christmas morning, Jimmy and Nick and Nana Fanny were surprised, but I wasn't. Mama wasn't. Mama and I are always holding our breath, waiting until the next time, whenever he decides that will be. Dad always finds us, arriving at the most inconvenient times, out of money and out of luck. It's always hard to get rid of him, and when he does finally leave we never know why, because he never bothers to say goodbye.

Mama has gotten good at keeping her distance from him, even when he's right there in the same room, but he still gets under her skin, which makes her hard to be around. Even when he's close by, not necessarily in the same house but in the same town, she gets distant, bitchy, even weepy. "He tries to get his foot in the door," she says, "so he can squeeze all the way in and take over." She still loves him, but she'd never admit it. She probably can't help but remember what he was like when they first met. I wish I'd known that Taylor, the one in their wedding pictures, a clear-eyed, wiry, blonde, athletic guy—smart, funny, and from what I heard, full of big plans—instead of the Taylor I remember, always drunk or strung out, calling from jail and begging to be bonded out. What happened to make the good Taylor go bad? His badness must've been there all along, even when she met him. Right? Or at least the seeds of it.

A few years ago I asked Mama, when did he start going bad? Was it gradual, or all at once? Both, she said, which makes no sense. I asked her: What made him turn out to be such a loser? What were his parents like? She told me that they were rich, and that his mother drank and his dad was cold. But his sisters and brother all turned out normal enough—jobs, families. Maybe it was you, I actually told her. He married you and lost his marbles. She actually laughed at that, a sad little laugh, and shook her head. He was just good at pretending, she told me, and I fell for it.

Couldn't she have seen through the good guy mask if she'd tried hard enough? Did she miss the signs, or just not want to see them? She saw signs early on, she said, him liking to drink and smoke pot, and the fact that he dropped out of the University of Iowa, and quit every job he got because he wasn't going to "put up with the bullshit," but she thought that once they got married and had me, he'd want to do better. Be a better person. Of course that didn't happen. He got worse. Stealing from grocery stores. Trying to cheat landlords out of money by paying the rent later and later until he'd skipped a month. Stringing lots of women along. He probably has other kids all over the world.

So I asked her: Is he evil, or just screwed up? Did the drugs make him bad, or was he already bad? Is he capable of, like, killing someone? She said she didn't know what he was capable of, and that's what scared her the most. That's why she finally decided to leave him in New Zealand and bring me back to Iowa, where she got involved with—you guessed it! Another alcoholic. And after that, Gordon, much younger than her, who considered himself to be a shaman and took us to live on a commune in New Mexico. And so on. One selfish jerk after the other. Didn't learn her lesson, until maybe now, maybe with Jimmy. Maybe.

Bottom line: I don't want this to happen to me. I want to know what the signs of evil are and how to recognize them. I want to know, up front, what kind of guy I'm dealing with. That's why I watch those crime shows, like *Dateline* and *48 Hours*. So I can recognize a heartless bastard when I see one.

The jury is still out on TJ. He does some illegal things, but who doesn't? He's close to his dad, and works hard. He puts up with me and Nick. And he seems honest. *Seems* is the key word here.

I keep thinking of Mr. Creep in my photo. That blank, hard stare. He's one of the bad ones. He must've followed us back to the Frost Fair to see what we were up to. He didn't try to hide when I took the picture. He wanted to scare me. Warn me about who we are dealing with. But he doesn't understand who *he's* dealing with. I'm *used* to dealing with losers, a.k.a. Mama's boyfriends—guys with no conscience.

Hope that this time I don't have to do it alone.

Dad comes outside in the street with Nick and me. We set down the old beat up skateboards he gave us—probably he found them in a dumpster.

I can see my breath, but the sun's out. Dad sits down on the curb to smoke, under a palm tree. He looks like one of the homeless people who hang out down on the pedestrian mall. Nana Fanny had poured a shot glass of liquor into his coffee mug. Two peas in a pod, I can almost hear Mama say.

"I know all about skateboarding, so I'll supervise," Dad says in his gravelly voice. "You gotta have a motto so you won't feel bad when you fall."

"A motto?" I say, making it sound like the silliest idea ever.

Which didn't stop my dad from making one up. "Thrills and spills," he says. "How's that?"

Nick chants, "Thrills and spills, thrills and spills."

I don't say a word. I did enough falling when we were ice skating. And concrete's harder than ice.

"First thing," Dad says, "you gotta learn to push."

"You already tried to teach me how to do this," I remind him. "When I was in kindergarten. I scraped up the entire left side of my body. You probably don't remember."

"I do," he says, squinting up at me. Who knew whether he remembered or not? "I'm better at teaching now than I used to be."

"Uh huh," I say. I don't mention that, until I scraped myself up, I'd been having the time of my life on that skateboard.

"Show us. Show us," Nick says, kicking her board toward him.

"Nah," Dad says.

"Dad," I say. "Come on. You know you want to."

He looks at me, grinning. Like I'd just given him the best present ever. He sets down his mug. He crushes out his cigarette under his floppy shoe. His shoes look like they came from the same dumpster he found the skateboards in. He stands up and positions the rattletrap board. The street is empty, new concrete, smooth as a shell that's been in the ocean for centuries.

He says, "I use a goofy-footed stance, left foot up and kicking with my right. You'll figure out what works for you." And he takes off, like magic. Graceful and free. So different than the skulking, apologetic creature who showed up on our doorstep earlier. He goes about a block and returns to us, smiling like a kid.

Nick retrieves her board and we set our wobbly contraptions down, take a deep breath together, and push off. We both fall on our butts, arms waving.

Nick shouts, "Thrills and spills."

I brush tiny rocks from my calf.

"Face your fear," Taylor says. "That's another one."

We get up again.

"Stay loose," Taylor says. "Defy gravity." He seems to have plenty of mottos handy. The ones I think of are "Family first" and

"Act your age," but I don't dump on him—he's just trying, in his own way, to be a dad. Also, it's a lot of effort to keep hating him, though God knows I try.

Nick and I push down the street and after a few pushes, I can feel my body pulling together, balancing crookedly, both feet up on the board, knees loose. Nick, too. We're skating like old ladies, but skating. Nick gets off at the corner and returns to Nana Fanny's house, but I practice pushing for one block more, staying low to my board. I don't give a damn how dorky I look.

When I get back to Dad and Nick, Sherry the policewoman comes out of her house. She heads toward her police car, like she's going to work, but she's wearing white jeans and a fuzzy green and red striped sweater, a huge leather purse slung over her shoulder. She's carrying a big straw tote bag full of presents. When she sees us she comes crunching down her oyster shell driveway in her high heels and tells us that we are breaking the law.

"Busted," Dad says.

Sherry ignores his humor. "Those things damage the street," she says.

"More than police cars do?" Dad asks her with his wide-eyed, innocent look. He's slouched on the curb, earring dangling, smoking a cigarette and slurping the last of his doctored-up coffee from Nana Fanny's Christmas tree mug. Looks like he just stumbled out of an all night party.

"And you are?" says Sherry.

Dad introduces himself and sticks out his tattooed hand, which she grasps firmly and shakes. "It's my fault," he says. "I suggested they come out here."

"It's illegal to skate anywhere but a skate park," she tells us.

Nick and I stand there clutching our boards in front of us. She's going to arrest us, on Christmas morning?

But she smiles and waves her hand. "I'm headed to my honey's for brunch," she says. "You gals be careful."

"You get to drive that patrol car even when you're not working?" Dad says. "Cops get all the breaks."

"I've got a shift later." She glances down at Dad. Her turned up nose makes her look less tough than she acts. "You're welcome to ride along with me so you can see just how much fun it is."

Dad shakes his head. "Tell your honey Merry Christmas!"

After she drives away, Nick says, "Let's go teach Haiku his puzzle." She sounds nervous.

But Dad says, "No, man. What're you waiting for? The wicked witch is gone. You'll never be champions unless you practice."

"Can you teach us more?" Nick asks Dad, just trying to be nice. She probably feels sorry for him.

"Ya'll just need practice." He waves us away. "I need another one of these here coffee drinks. Carry on." He gets to his feet, stretches, and heads back toward Nana's house. "Be right back!" he calls over his shoulder.

Yeah, right.

I tell Nick about the picture of Mr. Creep at the Frost Fair.

"Oh my God! We should tell Sherry," Nick says when she and I are headed back down the street again. We have to speak up over the clack-clack-clack of the wheels.

"Definitely," I say, but right then all I can think about is Dad, and how much I wish he wasn't here, and how guilty I feel for wishing that, especially on Christmas.

Dad asks to be dropped off at the pirate hostel, where they serve pancakes in the shape of skulls and crossbones. He jabbers the whole way to the hostel about how cool Coquina Bay is and how he knows he can get a job here, blah blah blah. After he gets out, we head back to the B&B. Nick and I spread out in the backseat and I can breathe again.

Mama says, "I am exhausted. Emotionally. Exhausted."

Jimmy says, "It'll be fine."

Mama says, "I shouldn't have asked him about the land in Washington. I knew better. Ask him a simple question."

Jimmy says, "It'll be fine." He squeezes her slumped shoulder. "I'll fix you a nice hot mug of passionflower tea."

"Uh huh." She sighs and droops her head. "Why does he have to ruin Christmas?" Another sigh.

I say, "Hey, Mama, let's watch some *Gilmore Girls*." After a hard day, Mama and I used to love to pop in a DVD of *Gilmore Girls*—we have all seven seasons and we've watched them countless times. They never get old. We would curl up together under an afghan with a bowl of popcorn and commune with Lorelei and Rory, because, like them, we were a mama and daughter against the world. We always watched it by ourselves, even when we were living with one of her choice men. But maybe it won't be so bad if Nick watches with us. Jimmy, I'm sure, would rather nail boards together.

"That sounds good," Mama tells me without turning around.

"I've never seen that show, but I'd like to," Jimmy says.

Well, whaddya know?

Nick says, "Taylor's gonna teach us to skateboard. He's really good." Nick starts chanting and I join in. "Thrills and spills!"

"I wouldn't hold my breath," Mama says. "He's got a history of moving on."

Back at the B&B, while Mama is setting up the *Gilmore Girls*, I chat on Facebook with Renda and tell her all about Mr. Creep and about Dad showing up. She's met Dad, so I don't have to explain. She tells me that her family served Christmas dinner to homeless people at the shelter. *I kept thinking about your dad the whole time we were there,* she writes. *I'm glad he was with you and not, you know.*

It takes a few minutes before I can type back, *Me too.*

But Dad doesn't move on, not right away. The day after

Christmas he shows up in front of our house, on foot again, wearing a clean t-shirt but the same dirty jeans.

For lack of anything better to do and anyone else to do it with, Nick and I are skateboarding down the driveway, practicing turning onto the sidewalk at the bottom of the hill. We want to go to the skate park, but not until we won't totally embarrass ourselves.

Dad makes a big phony fuss about how good we've gotten on our boards. Then he holds out a couple of tickets.

I take one. "The Sheriff's Ghost Tour," I read out loud. It's widely known in Coquina Bay that the ghost tours are a complete rip-off.

"I got a job working for this Sheriff dude," Dad says. "Filling in, over the holidays. Told him I used to be an actor. Did my impressions of George W. Bush and Obama."

"Were you an actor?" Nick asks.

"Sort of."

Who knows what that means?

He tells us that the job requires him to dress up like a deputy and give tours on Tuesday and Wednesday nights, the slow nights. Tomorrow night is his first shift, and he wants Nick and me to come.

"But my slumber party!" Nick whines. "I can't go tomorrow."

"I don't think Mom'll let us anyway," I say. Mom hasn't let me go anywhere alone with Dad since I was eight years old and he took me into the Foxhead in Iowa City and forgot about me.

Dad ignores me. "You can come the day after tomorrow," he tells us. "Hell, you can come any night you want, long as I'm working. It's gonna be really cool. I had to learn their whole script, but I'm gonna improvise. Make it wild."

This I've got to see. Dad, leading a ghost tour. Dressed like a cop.

"Afterwards we can drop in on that police lady. Wouldn't it freak her out if I showed up in my deputy uniform and told her I'd joined the force?"

Nick giggles.

"You better not." My face, already flushed from skating, gets hotter. Nick doesn't know that Dad has been in prison for dealing drugs. That was a long time ago, but still. He doesn't need to be "freaking out" police officers.

Just then, Molly the alligator tamer pops out onto her front porch in stretchy Capri pants and a neon-yellow jacket, her running clothes.

Nick and I wave to her, and Dad waves, too. Thank God she just waves and starts off jogging the other direction.

Dad watches her go. "What's her story?"

I probably don't need to explain this. Dad will flirt with a stump, as Mama used to say. And he does more than flirt if he can. One of the many reasons she divorced him.

I tell Dad goodbye, tell him that we'll do our best to be there.

Jimmy and Mama are still painting, giving the library walls a second pale yellow coat. Nick and I already did our agreed upon painting this morning, and we don't want to be roped back in, but we have to risk it. We show them the tickets and tell them about Dad's new job.

Jimmy steps off the ladder, glances at the ticket and hoots.

"So," I say, "can we?" Trying to act like I don't care, but I really want to go. We'll go the night after Nick's party. "I'll take my camera and get some cool night shots. Maybe we'll see Bony and Creepo there," I tell Nick.

Mama, sitting cross-legged on the paint splattered newspaper, rolls her head around like she's in yoga class. Her eyes are closed. From the radio in the kitchen, classical music swells and fades. Yellow paint drips from her paintbrush onto her Keds. She's clearly fighting off an outburst. "I guess so," she finally says. "If you both go and stick together."

She's getting weak in her old age. We get out of that library quick as cats. But we don't go far. Without even agreeing to do it, we lurk around the corner, our backs pressed against the wall, eavesdropping.

Jimmy says, "Why do you think Luna keeps talking about that Bony girl?"

Mama says, "She wants attention. She wants us to get all involved in feeling sorry for some strange girl. That way she keeps the focus on herself. She's always been like that."

Jesus. That is so not true. Is it?

"That is so not true!" Nick whispers.

I put my finger to my lips.

Jimmy says, "We need to do some things with the kids. Go to the movies. Or the skate park. I need to get back out on the road with Luna."

"After New Year's," Mama says.

Sound of the ladder scooting.

Then: "There's got to be a waiting list for those ghost tour jobs," Jimmy says. "How the hell did *he* get one?"

"That man bullshits his way through life," Mama says. "And he's good at it. Why do you think I married him?"

"He's can't be *that* good at it. He *is* living out of his car. And he lost the best girl in the world."

I make a yuck-face at Nick. She sticks out her tongue—*gross*.

Mama says, "Why's he hanging around here? I don't trust him. He must be after something."

"Maybe he just wants to spend some time with Luna."

"He doesn't give a damn about her. He's already proved that."

"How're you feeling?" Jimmy asks her. "Any better?"

She doesn't answer, and I don't wait to hear anymore. I inch my way down the hallway on tiptoes and Nick follows me.

Eavesdropping—sometimes you find out more than you really want to know.

Chapter 7

Nick

The day after Christmas I go to the phone store and they transfer everything on my old phone to my new phone and Kat buys me a bright pink Body Glove for it. I get through that day playing with my new phone. I need space, I tell everyone. I'm back in my PJs, with a secret stash of chocolate drops that Nana Fanny gave me. I download free music apps and read the little bios on everyone. Chuck Berry—was he a bad guy or what? Put in jail for transporting a 14-year-old girl across state lines. Where were her parents? And how come when Dad plays "Maybelline" for me, he never mentions that? He's all *Chuck Berry and the Rock and Roll Hall of Fame* and *Chuck Berry and his move to Chicago* and *his lucky break when he met Muddy Waters.*

I stay in my room—listening to music, using up all my data that apparently belongs to Dad (he says). I pack an oilcloth bag with all the stuff—*accoutrements*—I want to take to the sleepover. I say the word out loud. In my life I hope to have plenty of accoutrements. I pack the bag three times. I'm definitely taking the Swiss chocolate bars. I can't make up my mind about whether to take my new PJs or yoga pants and a t-shirt. A robe? I usually wear my robe without a thought. Now I give it the critical once-over. It's from olden times. Covered with rosebuds. The pockets are frayed and it's too small, really. Every question is about whether they will like me. I hate thinking about that, but it seems to be in my blood: Will they like me? I don't even know if I like them.

After dinner I'm back in my room, searching for an app to find lost girls and eating miniature Kit Kats. The phone number if you want to report a missing child is 1-800-THE-LOST. The lost! I picture a throng of kids like a rock concert. Hoards of them. How did so many kids get lost? Who wasn't paying attention? I don't know why I keep going back to it. Once I had a toothache on a Sunday and could not go to the dentist. My tongue kept nipping into that tooth's tiny cavity. That's how I feel about Bony. She's like a sore place I can't keep away from.

The next day drags. I go for a haircut, a major production, anxiety all over it, and I hate my new haircut. It requires sticky goo to keep it looking right. After about ten minutes the sticky goo gets stiff. I feel like I'm walking around with thumbtacks sticking out of my head.

I repack the oilcloth bag.

I read.

I show Dad the app for missing kids and he says, "You don't need that." I say, "Too late," and "There're 800,000 missing kids every year." And he says, "Get focused on something useful." I know this tactic so well. He wants to *extinguish* my interest in Bony.

I go for my appointment with Louise. She looks tanned from Miami. She looks like someone in love. I so wish I didn't know that. I fill her in on Christmas, Luna's dad falling from the sky, and my fears about the sleepover. It's one of those sessions when I do all the talking. She's been gone for two weeks so I have to catch her up.

The. Day. Drags.

Until it rushes. Around four I start to have trouble breathing, I'm so anxious. I don't want to go to Maeve's, after all. I tell Kat. She's in the kitchen in an apron, looking through a cookbook the size of a birthday cake. I stare out the window over the sink while I tell her. I just don't want to say it right to her face.

"Sweetie," she says. "You've been looking forward to it."

"I changed my mind. Don't you always say that's what minds are for?"

Kat sneaks up behind me and puts her hands on my shoulders. She's gentle and that just kills me. "What would your mother say?" she whispers.

I scream, "Don't you talk about her." And then there's nothing left to do but charge out of the room. I've seen Luna do it often enough. Taking the steep stairs, I say, to no one in particular, "I'm going, I'm going, I'm going! Who wouldn't want to get out of this place!" And I remember Louise and geez, I think, I'll have to tell her about all this. That's the trouble with having a therapist. You can't screw up and just forget it. You have to re-hash the whole event. In detail.

So Dad drops me at Maeve Murphy's at six o'clock sharp, with my oilcloth bag of accoutrements and a sleeping bag that has cowboy scenes printed on it. A from-the-dregs-of-Dad's-life sleeping bag. It's bundled up with a stupid bungee cord. "Try to have a good time," he says.

"Yeah, right," I say. I don't know why I'm mad, but I'm mad.

Cool Maeve Murphy opens the front door. She's dressed in yoga pants and a stretchy yoga top. She smells like graham crackers. "It's a spa sleepover," she says. "Come on in."

Spa sleepover? I feel this lump in my chest—the troll of anxiety resides there. I am the first one and that's awkward. I try to be a good guest. Manners have been stressed by Dad, my mother,

Nana Fanny, and Kat, so I sort of go on auto-pilot, asking about the yellow and blue fish in the aquarium, shaking hands with her geek dad at his computer, waving to her mother as she carries loads of goodies from the kitchen to their family room. Maeve does this thing where she makes me feel special—an insider—because I'm there first. She gets out her list and we go over the activities: virgin margaritas, a taco bar, karaoke, pedicures and facials.

"Oh, God," I say, under my breath.

"What?"

"It's the pedicures."

Maeve holds her foot out and admires her old polish, sparkly magenta. "It's so sexy," she says.

What do I care for sexy? I can't stand the idea of guys staring at me and deciding if I'm sexy. Makes me want to crawl into a hole. What she doesn't know and what no one knows except maybe Luna is that I still bite my toenails. It started when I was four and bendy as Gumby. And now I'm fourteen and not so bendy, but I still manage to bite my toenails. I always cover my toes. Even at the beach—I wear Crocs. In fact, I brought winter house slippers with me tonight, goofy fluffy house slippers with little duckbills on the toes.

I am cornered.

Somehow I did not think sleepover meant "all about your body."

I feel the way I did right after my mother died when I stopped brushing my hair. And my dad sort of forgot to brush it, too, and I grew serious rats in my hair. The teacher came to my house and talked to Dad about it. She had to shake us out of our grief. I cried for hours after that. That's when I truly understood the word humiliation. And it creeps up on me now, the potential for extreme and possibly permanent humiliation. I am thinking I will take a shower or something while the pedicures are happening. Or maybe I'll need to call home: Kat's ploy. I could always get fake sick and go next door to Nana's. I can tell you right now what Louise would think of that.

The doorbell starts ringing. On Maeve's computer there's a YouTube video of Selena Gomez blaring. Not my favorite. I keep wondering when she had surgery on her lips to make them so puffy. She's hula-hooping in the video. I pretend it's fascinating, beyond the beyond. When, really, I never even liked her on *Barney* reruns.

Girls with all their girl gear arrive. It's chaos. Everything is cute, cute, cute. Shrieking, over-the-top chaos. Chaos I try to disappear into. How I wish Luna were here. She usually has stuff to say and I can go mute like I did when I was in pre-school and my mother would pick up the slack and actually *speak* for me. Then someone—someone new, Alicia, super-tall, a basketball player—asks to see my new phone and we talk about apps. Karaoke. Tumblr. Words with Friends. She downloads Words with Friends and we sit side-by-side playing. I almost forget about cataloguing the food out the corner of my eye: corn chips in a humongous bowl, three kinds of salsa, tamales and churros, chocolate covered strawberries. Maybe it'll be all right.

We eat in the family room and her mother has the sense to disappear after all the food is laid out on the counter. Maeve puts on a white apron and mixes the virgin margaritas. Toasts all around. The margaritas are like gummy sours. I try not to pig out. I want to. Kat says you are what you eat—why she hasn't become a cinnamon roll, I just don't know.

It's nearly dark and out the windows I see the lights in Nana's house next door, golden little boxes. I wish for a second I was there. With Haiku. On the bed watching movies and eating popcorn Nana makes in the wok. Louise says I have to take brave steps to traverse my teenage years without my mother. Louise, it's a step—a spa sleepover where I'll be forced to sing karaoke and get a pedicure on my raggedy toenails. Two things I never thought I'd do. At what age are you allowed to stop doing what other people expect of you? I tuck away that question for the next time I see Louise.

Some girls I recognize and know something about. Caroline Rex—with the pool, the mother with the Gerber daisy tat, the dad who does dog tricks. Maeve Murphy herself. Wendy Chang: wicked smart, very religious, a friend of Maeve's since kindergarten. Alicia, wearer of lipstick who likes word games. There's lipstick on her front teeth. She's totally not cool—she's real—and I figure that's why she picked me out of the crowd. Peas in a pod. Beyond that, I am gathering all kinds of verbal and non-verbal information. I hear someone say, "She's so ghetto," but I don't know who they're talking about.

Maeve's mother steps in, flicks the lights and says, "Dad and I are going out to eat. Call us if you have any issues."

Issues? It's as if all the girls hold their breath until we're sure the parents are gone. Their headlights bob down the driveway.

In her let's-get-down-to-business tone, Maeve says to Wendy, "Let's see it."

Wendy gets into her duffle bag and pulls out a huge purple book—*The Joy of Sex*. She opens the book on a round coffee table and we gather around. She says she stole it from the closet of her dead American grandmother. She wants us to know that her Chinese grandmother would never have owned this book. She'd die if she even saw this book. But not Wendy. Wendy shows us the penis in all its glory. The man and the woman are both quite hairy. She says according to the author sex is all about friendship and tenderness. That's a news flash. I picture Luna and her guys in the library of the B. That doesn't look like friendship to me. It looks like they are shoplifting from each other. Where's the joy?

Wendy turns to the index and finds the page numbers for masturbation. She would be a good school librarian. She reads to us.

"Boys can't stop it," Caroline says.

"They do it all the time."

Caroline says, "My cousin calls it walking the dog."

"How do you know he's not just walking the dog?"

"Duh. No dog!"

"Girls do it, too," Alicia says. Uh-oh. So that's why she likes me. Takes one to know one is an expression Nana Fanny uses. I get it.

Much chattering, much denial. Much expression of being grossed out.

From the heights, Alicia bravely, foolishly, says, "I do it."

The circle widens around Alicia. She takes out a pack of gum and offers me a stick. I don't know what to do. Oh, I know what Louise would say. But what would I say? Time seems frozen. I know I'm hoping for karaoke now or that maybe Maeve's mother might have forgotten something and she'll surprise us, change her mind about going out to dinner, and bring out Maeve's baby pictures. Anything to change the subject. We need adult supervision is what I feel.

Alicia is wearing sweatpants that fit her too loose. Her t-shirt says Clean-Air Gardening; it's a shirt she got free when her dad bought a push mower. Her ears are pierced in three places. Those teeth with the lipstick? They are like crooked gravestones. But she has the most beautiful hair, French braided, and a fruity smell emanates from it, as if she's rinsed it in apple juice. And her toenails are perfect shimmery pearls. I'm judging her just like I don't want to be judged.

I say, "I do, too." It comes out sort of weak and crippled sounding. Not at all what I want. I move a few inches to Alicia's side. I'm terrified of Twitter now.

Maeve claps her hands and shouts, "Time for facials!"

Chapter 8

LUNA

The day after the day after Christmas, Nick holes up her room, no doubt snarfing candy. I wander around the house, out on the porch, back in again. All the workers are on holiday break. I miss TJ. Bethany calls and leaves two messages, which I delete. I call TJ and leave a message to see if he wants to spy on Mr. Creep's house later tonight. I get my skateboard out and scoot up and down the street, not going fast, stumbling and falling off only once. I keep my eye out for cops, but the streets are deserted. The other Victorians on Orange Street are all lit up, trees glowing, so cozy looking. The Sha-No-No, with its bare first floor windows, no Christmas lights, hardly any furniture, ladders and lumber visible, doesn't looking inviting, but I gotta go in sometime.

Jimmy is painting the trim in the music room. Paint stinking. Old rock music cranked up on his ancient boom box. He seems preoccupied—not humming or singing along with Creedence Clearwater—and doesn't speak to me when I walk right in front of him. He's been too busy to take me out driving.

He might be worried about Mama. I am. After breakfast today she announces that she doesn't feel up to painting. When I check on her, bring her some cookies, she's lying in their bed, staring out the window. She gives me a vacant little smile and says nothing's wrong except a headache. I've seen that vacant smile before, and I know better.

Mid-afternoon, Mama climbs out of bed, comes down to the kitchen in her robe and slippers and opens up the cookbook, and I'm thinking, okay, she's over it. But then Nick sidles into the kitchen whining about not wanting to go to the slumber party she's been jabbering about for days. Mama, trying to give Nick a pep talk, mentions Nick's dead mother. Nick bites Mama's head off and storms upstairs shrieking like a banshee, putting all our resident ghosts to shame. From the dining room, where I'm camped out with my laptop, I see Mama's shoulders droop and all the resolve goes out of her. Damn Nick.

Mama fries up lamb burgers—veggie burger for Nick—in the cast iron skillet, calls us to dinner and sits down and eats with us, but she's just going through the motions. She's not really here.

Nick doesn't notice, because she's decided to go to the party after all, surprise! Not even aware of all the tension, she blabs on about who's going to be there, like we know any of those people, like we care. Jimmy puts his head down, eats fast, and excuses himself to get back to painting. Mama just sits at the table while I load the dishwasher and clean up the kitchen.

Rinsing the thin china plates, I talk about the Sad Girl photo project. "I've *got* to find Bony," I say. "It's like she's trying to communicate with me. Her eyes. In that picture I took at her house. That's why I have to seek her out, take more pictures. Figure out what's going on with her." Once I explain this to Mama, I know it's true. I'm not just trying to get attention and keep things focused on me. I want to help Bony. I hope Mama will respond, but all she says is, "I see."

And I'm thinking, who's she mad at? Me for slutting around? Dad for showing up and ruining Christmas? Or did Mama and

Jimmy have a fight? Do they regret moving here and sinking all their money into this house? Has she changed her mind about being chained to a B&B? Do they regret getting married? All of the above?

I've got to find out soon, because this place feels even more haunted than usual. I should be out on Dad's ghost tour right now, but of course I have to wait for tomorrow night because of Nick.

I was hoping TJ would text me back, but who was I kidding?

I've got to get Mama out of here and let her talk and pump her back up again. The thought of playing therapist to Mama makes me feel tired and put upon, but I tell myself to buck up and get on with it. I've done it a million times.

So I propose a trip to Target. In spite of hating box stores in general, Mama loves Target. Also, Renda sent me a Target gift card for Christmas, and I tell Mama there's stuff on sale there that I gotta go see. Like that, I talk her into it. Just her and me.

Super Target is packed, even at night. People returning Christmas gifts they hate. Kids running around, ignoring their parents. Everyone's got a cart full of crap. The fluorescent lights are too bright, the store too red and too huge, the ginormous photos of perfect people in Target clothes too scary.

Mama and I arrange to meet at the in-store Starbucks in half an hour, and Mama wanders off to look at kitchen stuff while I lose myself in junior clothes, wishing Renda were here to give me advice. I find some cute kilt-like skirts (not wool, never wool in Florida) and cotton sweaters and t-shirts, none of them on sale, but who cares. I'm gonna branch out from jeans and tees. I try on the clothes, pay for one outfit—blue and green plaid mini skirt, orange cardigan sweater, white long-sleeved tee—and order a tall mocha at Starbucks. I stake out a table for two near the huge window facing the parking lot. Shoppers, looking like green zombies under the arc lights, are still streaming into the store.

Finally Mama shows up, empty-handed. Watching her sit down, I notice how her gray sweatshirt and jeans hang on her. She's lost weight. She looked like this before she left Brad, ex-husband number two, the FSU history professor who wouldn't quit screwing his ex-wife. Mama told me in great detail about how she'd walked in on them having sex, told me all kinds of things I really wish I didn't know.

I figure she's dying to talk now but just hasn't gotten up the nerve. Or something. I go to the counter and order her some green tea, her favorite, and figure why beat around the bush. I ask her what's going on.

She sighs, sips the hot tea from her paper mug. How can she drink green tea when the espresso and chocolate smells are so tempting? That's Mama for you.

Sitting two tables away is a couple I recognize from CBHS. They don't recognize me, probably. They are dressed up, she in a glittery dress and high heels, he in a button-down dress shirt, like they are on a date. Too much product in their hair. A date, at Target? The guy says, "I can do ten back flips in a row."

Mama hasn't answered, so I ask, "Is it Dad?" It's the safest place to start. Better she's mad at Dad than at Jimmy.

She shakes her head, no, no. She has more silver strands in her hair than she used to, and her shag cut has gotten too shaggy. "It's just…I know I've been preoccupied."

"Is it the house?" I drain the dregs of my mocha. I could drink two more.

The guy at the next table is swiping through photos on his phone, showing certain ones to his date. One of them is his ex-girlfriend, he proudly announces. Isn't she hot?

"I love the house, honey."

"You're tired of Jimmy."

"I'm crazy about Jimmy. He is a tight wad, but that's better than the alternative." She actually smiles, a little smile.

"Nick's a brat."

"We'll work it out." Mama takes another sip of tea. "I haven't been feeling well. I'm not supposed to tell you."

I get a horrible icy cold rush. "You're sick. You have cancer."

She sets her tea down and I look right into her eyes, those ever-so-familiar hazel Mama eyes, and I feel my blood start to flow again. "I'm healthy as can be," she says. "Okay, here goes." She shrugs her shoulders and looks almost embarrassed. "I'm pregnant."

"What? No way! You're, what, forty-five."

The teenage couple have stopped talking and are just sipping their frappes. I hope to God they aren't listening.

"I *know*," she says, widening her eyes and leaning toward me. "I can't believe it. You know I've been in peri-menopause for a few years. I still get my period every now and then."

Yuck.

"I recently started getting symptoms. Breast tenderness, tiredness, queasiness. Feeling all-over sensitive."

Yuck yuck yuck.

"So I took an HPT, which was positive, but I still thought, huh? I'm forty-five! Went to the doctor. I am four months along."

"Shit!"

She sighed again. "Shit, indeed."

"I'm sorry. I mean, congratulations. Wow."

"Wow. Yeah."

I have so many questions. I don't know where to begin, but Mama doesn't wait for me to figure out what to say.

"Jimmy doesn't want anyone to know yet. He can't process it. He's worried about how Nick will react. She's been through so much." She reaches over and squeezes my hand.

I nod. Haven't we all?

"I *am* starting to get excited about it," she says in a low voice. "I mean, what a gift, right? Jimmy will come around. How do you feel about a little sister or brother?"

"Okay, I guess. Fine. Great!" What else am I going to say? I blurt out, "What about fixing up the house? Running the B&B?"

"Jimmy's worried about all that."

I can see why.

"Just please. Don't tell Nick. And don't let Jimmy know that you know. For right now. Okay?" She stands up and gives me a hug, and I hug her back, hard, tears springing to my eyes. God. Now what?

The couple next to us is gone, and I didn't see them leave.

The following night is the ghost tour.

I've promised myself I'll act normal if it kills me. I can't decide how to feel about a new baby. It's going to change everything. What if Jimmy wants to call it quits? What if the baby has a birth defect? Bottom line: I hate having to keep such a big secret. Hate.

After dinner Nick and I bundle up in actual coats, gloves, and scarves. I put on my fleecy flap hat and Nick dons one of Jimmy's stocking hats and we set off for downtown in the dark. Even with all our precautions, the damp cold sinks into our bones and makes us shiver. We tromp along in the street so we'll be right under the streetlamps. The town is so dead that our boots sound loud on the pavement.

"Wonder if anyone else will be on the tour," Nick asked.

For some reason, since I know what's coming and Nick doesn't, I feel a little protective of her. "There better be. It'll be weird if it's just Dad. And us."

"Or us, Taylor, and Mr. Creep and Bony."

"A ghost tour is exactly where the Creep might take Bony."

"Man," Nick says. "The Creep could be watching us right now."

We quicken our steps and break into a run, sprinting the last block to St. James Street. Ever since I showed Nick the picture of

Mr. Creep at the Frost Fair, she is petrified of running into him. But we still talked about helping Bony. We just haven't figured out how to do it. I keep wanting to involve TJ, which makes Nick roll her eyes.

There are three suckers waiting in front of the tour office, a small storefront on St. James Street, the pedestrian mall. A bigger-than-life-size cardboard cutout of the Sheriff, a Tim McGraw look-alike, is propped up beside the door.

I say, "Does he look like someone you'd trust?"

"Not in a million years," Nick says.

The three other people are two middle-aged women and a guy who looks to be in his early twenties. The women are wrapped up in so many clothes it's hard to see what they look like, but one wears glasses and one doesn't. The guy, a preppie type, doesn't even have a jacket on, just a t-shirt and shorts and flip-flops, like it's August. He's talking, really loud, to the women, about the cool shrunken heads in the *Ripley's Believe It or Not!* Odditorium. Shrunken heads. And the babies in jars. Which makes me think of Mama's baby, all pickled in a jar, sitting on a shelf in the library. I'm a sicko.

Out steps Dad, all duded up in black pants, a black vest and jacket, plus a white shirt with a black string tie and a big black cowboy hat. A tin star pinned to his vest. I want to howl with laughter, but I keep from it by not looking at Nick. I whip out my camera and snap his picture.

"Welcome folks," Dad says, in a very un-Dad like voice. "Welcome to America's oldest city. I'm Deputy Lonnie Pritchard, and folks, I'm a ghost. I was shot by robbers here in Coquina Bay one tragic night along with the local sheriff, but I'm back tonight to tell you some absolutely true stories about strange goings-on here in Coquina Bay."

"Is this tour as good as the *Ripley's*?" the preppie boy asks Dad. His voice is a little slurry.

"Son, what's your name?"

"Umm." Like he can't remember. "Nathan."

"Well, Nathan. Here's the deal. If, at the end of this tour, you aren't frightened out of your wits, I'll refund your entire fifteen bucks."

Nathan grins. "Hell, yeah!" He staggers sideways. Uh-oh. There are lots of overpriced bars on St. James Street, or so Bethany told me.

The woman with the big square glasses says, "Oh, this'll be fun!"

"Four Eyes," I whisper to Nick.

Her friend wears a pink angora scarf wrapped twice around her neck like a big collar. "We're professional ghost people," she says. "We're with Ghost Hunters of Capps, Florida."

"Pinky," Nick whispers to me.

"Well now," Dad says. "Two believers and one unbeliever."

"Hey, I believe," says Nathan. "I just don't think you can scare me."

"What about you, young ladies?" Dad says. "I'm surprised your mother let you come out by yourselves on such a night!"

"We believe in ghosts," Nick says. "We want to see some."

"We're here because you asked us to come," I say. "Dad."

He laughs, and so do the other guests.

We start off to look for ghosts, but what we find is much worse. Did I mention that Coquina Bay is scary at night?

Chapter 9

NICK

Taylor's black sheriff's hat has a ketchup stain on the brim, but his badge looks real. Around the corner, on a dark side street, he goes into some long hot-air number about a woman who'd hung herself on the top floor of the college dorm when it was still a hotel, and how college students to this day see a figure hanging in that room, etc.

Pinky and Four Eyes are thrilled and ask tons of questions.

Luna whispers nervously to me, "He's making this up."

Maybe not, I'm thinking. She might have been bullied. She might have felt a stain all over her body—humiliation in the extreme. And when you feel that, you think it will never go away.

Four Eyes punches his answers into her iPhone. Could Taylor get in trouble with Ghost Authorities?

Four Eyes says, "What was the name of the girl who woke up and saw the ghost hanging in the middle of the night?"

"Mary Catherine Walsh," Taylor says. "And the year was 1972."

Nathan isn't so impressed. "Shit, man, that sounds like something out of a TV movie," he says. "Somebody offing herself. Who cares? Hit me with something scary. You're livin' in the zombie era."

"Young man," says the prim ghost-buster lady Pinky. "We're on this tour for research purposes, and we'd appreciate it if you'd behave yourself."

"You've got to be freezing," Four Eyes scolds. "You don't have enough clothes on."

"What is this—kindergarten?" Nathan says.

"You can always leave," Luna says, a lilt in her voice, like she surprised herself.

Nathan throws up his hands. "Hey! Back off, girls."

"Settle down, folks," Taylor says. "Don't upset the deputy if you know what's good for you. Next I'm taking you to a haunted bed and breakfast where a horrible double murder occurred."

"Oh goody," says Pinky and she adjusts her pink scarf so that it pools around her face like an inner tube.

There are at least a dozen B&B's in Coquina Bay, but naturally Taylor turns and heads straight for the Sha-Na-Na. Is this really on the tour? Or is he trying to scare me and Luna? I want to trust him, but Luna doesn't. Why would I? She's so skittish around him. Push-pull. Love me, don't. I plan to tell him to fuck off if he makes her cry. It'll be my first time. I practice saying it to myself. Other girls do, but I keep thinking my mother will know and, according to Louise, I'm sort of stuck at the age I was when my mother died. Saying fuck off, I think, will bring me up to fourteen or more and impress the hell out of Luna.

The B is a few blocks away. By the time we get there I'm frozen and want to leave the tour and disappear inside. To my stash of candy and my safe bed and my books and my apps. I need to distract myself. It's been twenty-four hours since I submitted my feet for a pedicure and met Maeve's big brother, Joe. Fortunately Alicia did my pedicure. She has five younger sisters and said she's seen all kinds of feet. She told me to sit still six times. She made my feet look almost normal. But then I got dragged into karaoke. I did

"Hey Jude," and I stank in the extreme.

I went upstairs to the bathroom and a boy stuck his head out a bedroom door and said hi. Joe Murphy. We talked about dogs and apps. After the sex book, I tried not to picture him with his dick in his hand. He was watching a forensics TV show and where he paused the screen was all bloody. For some reason, I told him about Bony—it was something I had to offer. We accomplished all this in seven minutes. In the early morning, I packed up my oilcloth bag and went over to Nana's.

But about *The Joy of Sex*, I keep remembering Alicia saying that she does it and me saying that I do it, too. And the way the other girls sort of backed off and started talking to each other in these bright, phony voices. Alicia and I were stuck like glue for the rest of the night. And today Caroline Rex sent me a text that said, "Don't feel bad, but we might not be friends. It doesn't feel that comfortable."

Don't feel bad?

Am I supposed to buy a bag of confetti and celebrate? It's been twenty-four hours. Who else will I hear from? For about the fiftieth time this school year, I consider running away. Running away and starting over where no one knows me or that I do it like a boy. Like, all the time. I'd try California or Iowa. Kat's told me a lot about Iowa. It sounds cool.

I'm thinking all this, distracting myself with self-loathing, wondering about Joe Murphy and whether he would still talk to me if Alicia and I are denounced as sluts and perverts when school starts up. Daydreaming on a ghost tour is not advisable. I trip on the same bit of upturned sidewalk that I tripped on my first day in Coquina Bay. But this time it really hurts. I feel a trickle of blood on my hand.

"I'm bleeding," I say to Luna.

"Do you want to go home?"

The B is big and grand in the dark because you can't see the peeling paint and rotten boards. The porch light's on. The TV flashes in the living room—the la-de-da parlor—where Kat and Dad are watching a movie by firelight. There's a light on upstairs, too…in one of the empty bedrooms. Why's that on?

Do I want to go in? Not really. And it seems like my life is like that now. Two choices, neither one all that appealing. Sometimes worse than that, a choice where I know there's a right and wrong, but can't tell the difference. I suck it up.

The ghost hunters and Luna and I draw close to Taylor. Nathan keeps his distance behind us, leaning against a live oak.

"Folks," Taylor says, "This house was once owned by the Vermillion family, 'round the turn of the century. Mr. Marcus Vermillion was a shipping magnate. Now folks, the Vermillions had two lovely teenage daughters, and in 1906, when the tragedy occurred, these girls were fifteen and fourteen."

Just like us, I want to say.

"They were said to be the prettiest girls in town."

Not so much like me.

Taylor goes on. "But few people had ever actually seen the girls, because their parents never let them out of the house. They went out every morning to church, very early, wearing hats and veils, so nobody could see their faces. They stayed inside the rest of the time. Young ladies, could you imagine living like that?"

"No!' I shout, but Luna barely smiles. She's holding back. Waiting to see where he goes with the story.

"Those two young ladies, Rosemary and Polly were their names, got fed up with being locked in the house. They tried to run away a few times but were always caught and brought back by their father's servants. But one night, in January of 1906, the two beautiful young ladies sneaked into their parents' bedroom, where they were sleeping, which was that lighted room up there, and they stabbed their mama and papa with butcher knives. The girls escaped after that and were never seen or heard from again. But everyone who's ever owned this bed and breakfast has reported hearing the mother crying late at night, and the father's footsteps pacing up and down the upstairs hall, waiting for their beloved daughters to return. If the light's left on in that room, the noises don't happen. But if, for some reason, that light goes out, then the noises return. And make no mistake, those are the noises of grieving parents. Doesn't matter to them they were murdered by their own children. Because, you see, they've forgiven them. They were only trying to protect those beautiful daughters the best they knew how. Only, I think we'd all agree, they went a little too far."

"You got that right," Nathan puts in. I can imagine him in elementary school. He probably hasn't changed one iota.

I tug on Luna's hand, puzzled. True or not true? I hate this story. It's not a story you should tell to a girl who's lost her mother.

"We'll find out," she whispers. "It's probably BS."

We've never heard anyone crying or pacing, but Luna did hear a ghost clearing its throat. Was that one of the Vermillions? What was with the light being on?

"That's a good story." Four Eyes with the iPhone is punching away again. "Vermillion, did you say?"

"You can read all about it in the local paper," Taylor says.

"Yeah, like I'll look it up," Nathan mutters. He's probably never even looked up a phone number in his life. Then louder, from his spot against the tree: "Let's see something totally wicked!"

Taylor faces us, walking backwards in the middle of Orange Street toward downtown. Like directing traffic, he wiggles his fingers for us to follow. His fake sheriff's badge glints in the lamplight. "There's been a rumor around town for years," he says. "A very bad thing happened once in the cemetery—where we're going next. I'm not supposed to tell you about it, folks, but tonight, since Nathan here is such a tough guy, I'm going to break the rules and tell you about the bad thing." He turns his back on us and strides off across the street.

"Cool!" I say. "Wait up, Deputy!" I am so faking my enthusiasm. And why?

I sort of get into a daydream about Taylor adopting me. I like that old car of his—a sky blue Rambler from the 60s. I wouldn't mind sleeping at the pirate hostel and eating skull-and-crossbones pancakes. He could teach me a few things about running away. Daydreaming on a ghost tour—not the smartest thing. You can trip on a cobblestone or end up lost in the graveyard.

The ghost hunters giggle, and Nathan harrumphs, but we follow Taylor. It's dark on the side streets, the street lights far apart, no moon or stars visible. Shops and restaurants we pass are lit up, late diners enjoying the warmth and coziness. It hits me—I am an outsider. Lonely. Will I ever go into one of those restaurants happy? And what does happy mean to me? We make our way carefully over the uneven, slippery brick sidewalk.

In the cemetery, the ancient, gray tombstones lean slightly to the left or right, any way but straight. Outside the iron fence, the streetlight doesn't feel like much protection. Protection from what? I decide that I do not believe in ghosts. Not this kind.

I know something about ghosts and when someone who's died visits you, it's not like Halloween or something you see in the movies. My mother came back to me. I'd see these wispy movements in the kitchen when I was getting ready for school. They were the color of her turquoise chenille bathrobe. Okay, maybe I do believe in Luna's hallway ghost. But either way, Taylor is no doubt going to make up something good to scare Nathan. I can't wait to see what it is. Mostly I want to get rid of my lonely feeling. I want to be shaken and shocked.

He glances around the graveyard, then turns to us. "Okay, here they come. Folks, see those people walking down that sidewalk there?" He points at a big person and a child walking hand in hand on the other side of the cemetery. Just shadows from where we stand.

"That man there," Taylor says, "is a murderer. He sneaks down this street every night at this time, looking for victims."

"Is he a ghost?" Four Eyes says quietly.

"Folks, that man there is deceased. Yes, he is a ghost," Taylor says. "The child is his latest victim. She is a ghost, as well."

"Lord have mercy," says Pinky.

"Those aren't ghosts!" I say.

Taylor winks at me.

"I think they are," Luna says.

"But they are wearing contemporary clothing!" hisses Four Eyes.

"The last death was only four years ago," Taylor says.

"So real looking," Pinky says. Then she shivers.

"Is this the bad story you promised?" Nathan says, not so smart-alecky now.

The man and the child turn toward us, walking in the street now. The child trips over a brick and the man catches the child by the hand. In the foggy night they do almost look ghostly—dark, bundled-up shapes—as they come toward us, but I know Taylor has been hoping they wouldn't turn toward us, because, well, they are as alive as we are.

"We'd better hide!" Taylor beckons us behind a large mausoleum and we all sidle over and tuck ourselves behind it. Nathan leans on the mossy wall. He seems to need support to stand. "Why do we need to hide from ghosts?" he says, too loudly.

"Would you like to meet him?" Taylor says in a soft, seductive voice. "I can call him over."

"This is too weird," says Pinky. She clears her throat, an old-lady hacking sound. "I didn't sign up for anything like this."

I squeeze the stuffing out of Luna's arm. She whispers to me, "It's just improv."

"For sure?"

"He's unpredictable," she whispers. "But I want to see what he'll do next. Story of my life."

Luna steps out from behind the mausoleum just when the man and the child pass under the streetlight. She sucks in her breath and jerks me to her side. It's Mr. Creep and Bony, of course. We can't go anywhere without them. We can't have an ordinary life anymore. He has a stocking cap on, but his ponytail hangs out the back. Bony wears a shiny ski parka with the sleeves too short. Cute as a button, as usual. I swear I can't breathe.

"Excuse me, sir," Taylor stage-whispers to Mr. Creep. Not so he can really hear. "It's Lonnie Pritchard speaking, a kindred spirit who also haunts these streets. There's a fellow here from the world of the living that wants to meet you, up close and personal. Name of Nathan. He doesn't believe you're a murderer. Or a ghost. Come let him have a look at you."

"What the hell?" Nathan says. "You're crazy." He staggers backwards, then darts off farther into the cemetery and disappears. Totally tipsy.

"No refund for him," Luna says.

Mr. Creep and Bony, having briefly paused, speed up again.

If she is kidnapped, they don't try to hide it. Luna grabs my hand and we run after them, leaving the tour behind and scrambling to get itself back together. Taylor didn't do a very good job, but this isn't the time to say so. I sort of think it should be like a school presentation. Who knows how much time he's spent in school. My heart's thudding. We turn onto a narrow street with palm trees rustling and restaurants lit up all golden. We get behind some guys in a band, carrying their black instrument cases. One says, "Whoa, girls!" But we zigzag around them. Mr. Creep and Bony are nowhere to be found on the street. Next to an alley, we sit down on the curb to catch our breath. Loud music comes from a tavern. I think I can smell the ocean, but it might be fish leftovers in the dumpster next to us.

"What're we doing?' I say. My voice is shaky. I'm the one about to cry.

Luna pulls her camera out of her jacket pocket. She says, "You keep saying we need evidence."

"I do not! I don't want to get involved! And you know what— my mother doesn't want me to get involved."

"Yeah—how do you know?"

"She told me so."

"If she was such a good person, why wouldn't she want you to? If she was such a good person—"

"Shut up!" I'm shivering like crazy. My knees are jerking like they did when I had to give a speech at school. Dad says it's called sewing-machine-knee.

The restaurants have balconies hanging over the street. I glance up and there they are. From where we sit on the curb, Mr. Creep has a long, horse-y face. They have snagged a balcony table. A big orange heater looms over him. He hogs the heat. They sit across from each other. Bony seems to watch us, but I don't think she can recognize us under the scarves and hats. Her eyes are dead empty. Her hair's styled into ringlets. She does not have her jacket on and I bet her arms are all goose-bumpy.

I stare at the cobblestone street like the truth might be printed there. I want to face my fear, but Mr. Creep is too close for comfort. "We have to tell someone," I say. "Someone besides Dad and Mom." I don't usually call Kat that. It feels like tasting a new food. I sort of like it. But I'm scared to like it.

Luna says, "Let's get the hell out of here." She's squeezing my hand real hard.

Chapter 10

LUNA

Things have gone nutsy cuckoo around the Sha-Na-Na. We are due to open one week after New Year's Day. There are floors downstairs to be refinished, rooms upstairs to be painted, a kitchen to be remodeled. Mama says that she won't be painting or refinishing because the fumes give her a headache—I know the *real* reason—so TJ and his dad are hired to strip, sand and refinish the hardwood floors after they help Jimmy re-do the kitchen. The kitchen is getting new appliances and countertops, cabinets, and a bamboo floor, because Mama says she can't cook in that "70s hovel." She's a bit on edge.

A few days after Christmas, TJ, Jimmy, and TJ's dad, Artie, commenced smashing up the kitchen. The dust is tremendous but it looks satisfying to smash up a kitchen. They won't let me do it, though. I asked.

Instead, Nick and I are assigned to remove all the framed photographs and pictures in the hallway and bedrooms upstairs—the eight guest rooms. Mama instructs us to take down the pictures, taking care not to pull apart their dusty wooden frames, place them in plastic tubs and label the tubs, then pull out the nails. Boring.

In the hallway between my room and Nick's hangs the constellation of family photos from the early 1900s. Nick and I had glanced at all the photos before, and I'd even snapped pictures of them, but now we study them again as we take them down.

In one of the pictures a dark haired little girl with a silly angelic look on her face perches primly on a cushion. I tell Nick that the angel girl was her twin.

"You think it's true, the story your dad was telling us on the ghost tour?" Nick asks. She has to talk loud over the racket coming from downstairs. "About the Vermillion daughters?"

I shrug.

One photograph shows a portly man in a suit too big for him, sitting spread-legged in a chair, a little blonde girl, wearing a white hair bow, on his lap. "Maybe this is one of the Vermillion sisters. Rosemary. Or Polly," Nick says. "But she looks too happy. And the man looks too nice."

"No no no. Here they are," I say, holding out the picture of the two girls with the white bird.

Rosemary and Polly. Now I picture them, a little older than in this photo, maybe the same age Nick and I are now, dressed in old timey hats and coats and carrying suitcases, creeping down this very hall on a dark, moonless night. One of them would've been carrying a candle, or a lantern. The parents would've been splayed in their bed, bloody, stabbed to death. Had the girls bothered to wash up afterwards? They wouldn't have wanted to wake the servants. How could the servants not have heard the sounds of murder? How could daughters ever do this to parents, no matter how awful they were?

I picture the real Nick and me creeping down the hall with suitcases, leaving behind the scene of a crime, some awful crime that I can't even imagine. Where would we go? How would we live with the guilt? Would we stay together?

A loud bang downstairs startles me. The men in the kitchen

roar in approval. Then, scraping, dragging sounds as they pull something across the floor.

"I always wanted a little brother or sister," Nick says.

"Sorry you got stuck with me," I say, trying to be funny. I really want to tell Nick about the baby, but I've got no idea how she'd react. Or if she could keep a secret.

"Shut up," Nick tells me, but not meanly. She is still examining the picture of the bird girls. "No, this isn't them," she adds. "They have blonde hair."

"Who does?"

"Rosemary and Polly."

I snort. "How would you know?"

She snorts louder, imitating me. "That's the way I imagine them."

"Well, I imagine them with dark hair."

For some reason this strikes both of us as funny and we both begin to giggle and then guffaw. I laugh until tears squeeze from my eyes, the pent up emotion from all the shit that happened before Christmas and during Christmas and after Christmas draining out.

"Stop!" Nick says, doubled over. "I'll pee my pants." She hands me the photograph and staggers down the hall to the bathroom and slams the door, still laughing.

I lean back against the wall, taking deep breaths. Then the sound of laughter bounces down the hall again, this time coming from the guest room where Mama is washing windows. Mama must've caught the laughing bug from us. Knowing she's laughing lightens my heart even more. I wander down the hall and stick my head into Room 7, now empty of all furniture.

It's cold in there, and Mama's hiccupping laughter echoes. Dressed in a long sleeved t-shirt of Jimmy's and a paint-spattered pair of jeans, she sits cross-legged, leaning against the wall, bottle of Windex and wads of newspaper beside her. One hand covers her eyes.

"Mama?"

She whips her head up. Not laughing. Crying. "Oh. God," she says. "Sorry."

I tiptoe in and stand beside her. I don't know where to begin, so I say nothing. I want to mention the baby, but I don't think I'm supposed to mention the baby.

I stand there, letting her cry, giving her some space, or at least that's what I tell myself I'm doing.

Mama lets out a huge, shaky sigh. "I don't know," she says. "I don't know if we should've taken this on. Now I'm useless. And money is flying out the window." She sniffles and wipes her eyes. "We've already got guests booked."

You shouldn't have gotten pregnant. Haven't you ever heard of birth control? "I can help more," I say, trying to make up for my mean thoughts.

"Me too," Nick adds from the doorway.

She shakes her head. "Thanks, guys," she said. "There's just no way we'll get done on time. No way." She buries her face in her arms. "We're almost out of money. We need more antiques. The whole house needs to be re-wired."

I squat down beside her and give her an awkward one-armed hug, but she only buries her head deeper. "Go on," she mumbles. "I'll be okay."

Nick and I drift off, and without even talking about it, start down the hall toward the stairs.

"Damn it!" Mama shrieks. There's a clatter like she's thrown something.

I can't look at Nick. She's never seen Mama act this way, and I've only seen it a few times. Maybe it's baby hormones, but I can't tell Nick that. I hate for Mama to feel so bad and for Nick to witness it and think less of her. And tease me about it, or use it against us. Her dad is always so calm. I've never even seen him lose his temper.

But Nick says nothing about Mama's display and I say nothing about it and we end up downstairs in the kitchen.

TJ kneels on the floor, chipping at linoleum squares with a metal scraper. His sun-bleached hair is covered with white plaster dust. Even though I felt like crap three seconds ago, now I long to go over and drape myself on him and this desire makes me go hot and speechless. Hormones?

"Hey, surfer dude," Nick says. "Where's my dad?"

TJ turns and gives us his wide smile. Only his mouth smiles, though. His eyes look sad. Oh, those sad blue eyes. Why so sad? I know I can make him happier and I know I'm an idiot for thinking that I have a chance with him. "They went out to load some shit in the truck," he says.

"Language!" Nick says, half-kidding.

Out in the driveway, Nick and I help Jimmy heave parts of the kitchen into the bed of Artie's ancient Ford pickup truck. Pieces of the Formica counters, sections of wooden cabinets. It feels good to grunt and groan and heave and hear the crash. I decide to forget about photography and become a construction worker. Finally we finish and Artie drives off toward the dump and Jimmy and Nick and I stand panting in the driveway, brushing ourselves off. It's one of those bone chilling days that we've had too many of this winter. Coldest December on record for Florida, the weather chick says. When the sun's out it doesn't feel bad, but right then it's low in the sky.

"How're things going upstairs?" Jimmy asks us. I can't tell, by his wrinkled forehead, if he's angry or worried or what. Don't know him well enough to read his signs. Reading signs is important if your mother has had as many significant others as mine's had.

"Uh," Nick says, breathing out a little white cloud. She stares over into the neighbor's yard where their fat Bassett Hound sits in a sunny spot, watching us through the fence. She's opting out, letting me explain.

I tell Jimmy about Mama being upset, but I'm thinking, don't be mad, don't take it out on her, please please please, she didn't get pregnant on purpose. Did she?

"We *are* behind," he says. He takes off his work gloves and slaps them against his thigh. "We can probably afford more help." He squints over at me. "Think I'd better go talk to your mama." He smiles his crooked smile.

I smile back so as not to blubber like a baby.

Jimmy swats Nick with his gloves and heads back inside. Nick follows him, but I don't want to go back inside yet and face the attraction I feel for TJ and the sympathy I feel for Mama, and, oh yeah, all the work we have to do.

"See you, Rosemary!" I call to Nick.

On the top step of the back stairs, she raises her hand like she's clutching a hatchet. "Adios, Polly," she says, and the door swings shut behind her.

"Polly?" The voice comes from an apparition, a girl gliding up the driveway toward me. But it's only Bethany, dressed in a wool cap and a lime green down jacket. "Is that, like, your nickname?"

"Yeah," I say, because, how would I even begin to explain it? "What are you doing?" I don't say, *here*, but that's what I meant.

"I need to talk to you, 'cause…how come you won't let me explain? You never return my calls or my texts, and I have to tell you what happened about the movies."

"I'll tell you what happened. It was a lame movie. Nick and I sat and watched the whole thing."

"It was my mom's fault!" Bethany says. "She found wine in my thermos when I didn't wash it out quick enough and she grounded me and took away my phone and I couldn't call you. I'm really sorry. And I wanted to invite you to my New Year's party. Will you come?"

More sad eyes. Lots of sad eyes today. But Bethany's trying to look sad, overdoing it, while TJ hadn't been trying. He'd been trying to look happy. And Mama can never hide her feelings.

"Whatever," was all I could come up with.

"So," she says, posing like a model. "Can I see inside your house?"

"Right now?"

She smiles. Pink lipstick. "Yes! Now!"

"It's a mess. We're remodeling."

"Pleeeese, girlfriend?" She bounces on the tiptoes of her Ugg boots. "I've always wanted to see inside this house. After I heard those stories about the ghost sisters, you know, the ones that killed their parents."

"You believe that stuff?"

"Not really, but it's way cool."

I feel the tightness inside me loosening up a little. Maybe I've been wrong. Maybe she didn't stand me up on purpose. Maybe she isn't really that bad. Maybe she's even stopped drinking.

Just then the back door creaks open and Nick pokes her head out. "Dad and Kat want to talk to us."

"That your sister?" Bethany crows. "Hi, sister!"

It still feels strange that I have a sister. And soon I'll have another one! Or a brother. How weird. "That's Nick," I say to Bethany. "Be right there," I tell Nick.

Nick makes a face at Bethany's back and disappears inside the house.

I hug myself, rubbing my arms in their thin thermal sleeves.

"Hey, that's TJ's car out on the street, right?"

Okay, so *that's* why she is suddenly dying to see inside my house. Maybe that's why she stopped by in the first place. Before I can answer, TJ himself hustles out the back door, no coat, and lopes down the back steps, swinging his car keys.

"TJ, hey!" says Bethany. "What're *you* doing here?"

"Damned if I know," he says, but he salutes me. "See you tomorrow, Polly."

Bethany and I stand and listen to his car roar away. "Should *I* be calling you Polly?"

"Nope," I say, too abruptly. I remind her I have to go inside.

"Text me!" she says over her shoulder. "Or I'll text you!"

What Mama and Jimmy have to talk to us about, after they sit us down in the living room, is the fact that they are going to hire my dad, just for the next couple of weeks, to help finish up at the B&B. Mama has a pained expression on her face, and Jimmy looks all stoic, but they are both insane.

Jimmy tells us that Dad called earlier to report that, after the shenanigans he pulled on the ghost tour, hiding behind graves, scaring his customers half to death—just trying to liven things up— the ghost hunter ladies complained and that was the end of his new job.

Although she didn't say so, I know that Dad losing the job reminds Mama of the long list of other jobs he lost. Manager of a food co-op—busted for stealing food. Teacher at a private elementary school—fired after two mothers he was sleeping with got into a screaming match on the playground. Clerk at a bookstore —drinking on the job.

Mama always talks about the Christmas he gave pot as a present to everyone except children under twelve. He wrapped the baggies in festive paper and put bows on them. "Why stop at twelve?" Mama screamed at him. "Why not give it to infants in their formula?"

"Everyone we know breastfeeds," he said.

And that ain't the half of it.

After Jimmy explains why hiring Taylor to help at the Sha makes sense, I run upstairs to my bedroom and dive onto my bed.

Why do they keep letting Taylor into our lives, giving him more and more second chances? Mama knows better, but maybe because of the baby she's not thinking straight. And being the swell guy he is, Jimmy probably talked her into it. Is Jimmy really as nice as he seems? He doesn't know my dad. Hiring Dad will be like letting the snake into the henhouse, as my granddad used to say. Even for two weeks. He can cause all kinds of trouble in two weeks.

Chapter 11

NICK

Those girls are a misery train bearing down on me. Big, fat sloppy tears clot up in my throat. I can joke around with Luna, but it's all a front. Louise would call it my front-stage self. Sweetness and light, Dad would call it. But inside I feel like I'm about to be strangled. High school will be such an unbearable drag if I'm humiliated. I might have to do something drastic. Like beg to be sent to boarding school.

It's night. So late that I finally understand the word insomnia. I have eaten chocolate, read until my vision's blurred, and played solitaire on my phone. My period's about to come—my boobs are sore and the acne troll just dropped a bomb on my chin. Usually I feel like doing it when my period's about to come, but not now. I may never do it again. It's like those girls—in their puke green moisturizing masks—haunt me.

In the hall, the dumbwaiter grinds to life. I peek out. Luna's there, pulling the dumbwaiter cord. She's in some outfit she's trying on. Since dinner she's undergone a private makeover. It's like she's trying on a new life. A life that will be hers in two years when she can leave the B, leave me, leave her boyfriends, her would-be friends at school. Skinny, skinny jeans and jewelry up both arms like tattoos. High heels. And she's done something to her hair. It's coppery on one side. She puts a finger to her lips to shush me. Out of the dumbwaiter she lifts a cardboard box. She beckons me into her room.

Her room is lit by a stained-glass lamp and it throws off colored patches of light. She's clomping around in the high heels and I know right at that moment she will never skateboard again, not even to please Taylor.

"Let's tell Taylor someone stole the skateboards," I say.

"Brilliant!" she says, and I feel good. Or better.

I say, "What's in the box?" I picture my box—the one I never open, my mom's stuff. Would I ever share it with Luna?

She lifts the lid, presents it to me like she's on stage. In Kat's handwriting, the label reads: PHOTOS FROM OTHER INCARNATIONS. We get cozy on the bed. Luna has to half-kneel to reach into the box. She plops a pile of photos on the bed between us. There are so many, but I don't say anything.

"Mom always said she'd put these in a scrapbook."

"Why didn't she?"

"It's evidence."

"Of what?"

"Her mistakes, I guess."

I don't say, Like you? But I wonder: Did Kat get pregnant by Taylor on purpose? And why would she? If he's such a slacker?

"This is the house we lived in in Iowa." She shows me a photo with curly edges: a gray house almost buried in snow. "And here I am in my snowsuit." Tiny Luna, in a red snowsuit. She's on baby skis and she's waving her poles like magic wands.

"Who's this guy?" I nudge a photo out from the pile. A young guy with a big gut, wearing a western belt with a belt buckle as big as a Moon Pie.

Luna scrunches up her nose. "Gordon. Number Two. What a pain in the ass."

"How so?"

"Wolves were his *totem* animal."

"What does that mean?"

"He wanted to *be* a wolf."

"Weird."

"He used to call me his little-big girl in a creepy voice."

"Like Mr. Creep?"

"Maybe." She shivers. Then she gets up and paces the room, her hands clasped behind her back. "Did you ever wish you had a brother?"

"A big brother?"

"Just a brother."

"He could protect"—I almost say *us*—"me."

"I don't think I want a brother. Or a sister." Too late, she catches herself. "But you're okay, Nick."

"Thanks. I'm not okay. Not really."

"What'samatter?"

Her clock reads 2:11. The freaking middle of the night. I wish my mom were here, even a ghostly scrap of her chenille robe. I'd tell her. And I think about going back to bed and wishing her to appear. I'd tell her. But she's not here. And Luna is.

"This awful thing happened. At the sleepover."

Her face says murder! Rape! Mayhem! But I say, "I think those girls are going to smear it in my face when school starts."

"What?" She darts urgently to the bed and sits beside me. "You have to tell me. It'll affect me, too."

"Promise you won't tell Kat?"

"Promise."

Even though I think that promise comes much too easily, I spill the beans. "Long story short," I say, just like Kat. I am starting to imitate her. I give it to her straight: that I do it, that I admitted it, that the other girls—all except Alicia—acted weird that night.

"Jesus."

"I know."

"I thought you must have another secret beside Kit Kats."

I pound the pillow. "Stop! Here's another promise I need. You won't tease me about it."

"I'd never," she says, one hand upon her heart. "Those girls do it, too."

"How do you know?"

"Almost everyone does."

"But they'll say I'm a slut. And a pervert."

"Bitches."

"It's bad, isn't it?"

"We'll think of something."

And she does. We sift through the photos. She turns all the photos of Kat's guys upside down in their own pile. I *ooh* and *ahh* over Luna as a newborn with a squished-up face, Luna smearing her face with chocolate cake at her first birthday party, Luna learning to walk, Luna's wispy baby hair clipped into a red barrette. Luna, Luna, Luna: the star of it all.

I yawn. It's almost three. I feel sleep melting my bones. I'm cuddled up with her body length pillow. Josh Hutcherson's face is printed on the pillowslip.

Luna says, "I've got an idea."

"What?"

"You need a headline, a feat so astounding that those girls wouldn't dare humiliate you."

"Such as?"

She takes my hand. "Listen."

I can't believe she's holding my hand. "I'm listening."

"Now let me have my say. Don't talk until I'm done."

"Okey-dokey."

"My intuition is hammering away at me. We have to do something for Bony. I heard of another case like hers. If some people—in that case, police officers—hadn't used their intuition, that girl'd still be sleeping in a woodshed." She lets that sink in and then she says, "And giving him BJs whenever he wanted them."

"Gross."

"That's what I'm saying."

"You just want to impress your photography teacher."

"That is so *not* true. I want to protect Bony. Every time I think about that creep and what he might possibly do to her—I feel so... so..."

"So what?"

"Pissed, that's what." She finally kicks off her high heels and paces in her bare feet, an ankle bracelet tinkling. "Girls have to stick together."

I say, "You mean *we* have to stick together?" This feels like a new development.

"Absolutely."

Chapter 12

LUNA

Since Nick and I were up so late bonding, practically pricking our fingers and swapping blood, I try to sleep in, but there's so much racket downstairs I give up around eight and open up my laptop to check on what Renda and my old buds are up to. Today they are going to try out the new zipline at the Natural History Museum! Facebook is all about showing off even when you're pretending not to. Sometimes it sickens me, even when I can't look away.

Around nine, Nick rolls out of bed and yawns in my doorway, wearing yoga pants and her dad's old SeaWorld sweatshirt, looking as grumpy as I feel. Even her zit looks angry. She plops on my bed waiting for me to get dressed. There's no need to talk. In the wee hours we agreed upon our mission. Somehow, somewhere, some way, we will find Bony and save her from Mr. Creep.

But first we have to work on the house, and before that we have to eat breakfast, and before that I have to put on clothes. TJ is downstairs with Artie, clomping and swearing in the kitchen, but I'm too tired to even try to make an effort to look good. No skinny jeans for me. My track warms-ups from 8th grade are the best I can do.

Downstairs in the library, Mama, a scarecrow in her paint-spattered uniform, is perched on the love seat, sipping tea and flipping through a book of fabric swatches. She tells us that Jimmy has gone off to find Dad and offer him work. Then she clamps her lips together, resigned, tired. Maybe she didn't sleep much either. She does have plenty to worry about.

A baby. At her age. At all our ages.

Since there is no kitchen to speak of, Mama offers to take us out for bagels and lets me drive her Subaru station wagon, the lesbian mobile, we call it, since this particular type of car is popular amongst her lesbian friends.

I accelerate away from the safety of Orange Street and merge onto the bypass where cars are whipping in and out of strip malls and fast food parking lots and I'm practically draping myself over the steering wheel I'm so nervous. Nick cowers in the back, gasping whenever she thinks I'm going to randomly decide to wreck into another car.

Mama stares straight ahead and delivers a monologue in a monotone voice that makes my skin crawl. "Not too close. Not too fast. Time to start braking. Okay, watch out for that guy. Don't hesitate. Give it some gas. Signal. Signal. Speed limit is 35."

"Would you shut up? I know how to drive! Shut. Up. Already!"

"At least I'm not yelling," Mama says.

"Or jumping out of the car," Nick says, and snickers.

Mama snickers, too.

Ganging up on me.

"Wait until you start driving," I say to Nick. God, what a thought.

A red Dodge Caravan with Pennsylvania plates whips in front of me and stops short to turn into Target. I put my blinker on and smoothly pull around him. "See, I can drive, damn it!"

Mama pats my arm, but doesn't look at me. "Focus. Focus," she mutters.

My pits are sweaty. "I'll ask Dad to take me out driving," I say, pleased with the idea. "I bet he'd be a good teacher."

Mama doesn't react like I hoped she would. She's too far into Driver's Ed mode. She begins tapping on her window. "There's Einstein's. Get over. Signal and get over."

Nick squeals, covering her face with her folded arms.

"Oh." Mama exhales. "Check over your shoulder *before* you change lanes."

"Let me out," Nick says, voice muffled. "I'll walk from here."

"Asshole." I'm concentrating too hard to defend myself any better than that. I *am* a good driver, damn it, and I'm going to get better. And Dad's loosey-goosey enough to be the perfect teacher.

After breakfast Nick and I continue prepping the upstairs for painting.

When Jimmy and Dad come back around noon, Dad looks sober and acts all quiet and grateful. It's a well-rehearsed schtick, his fake bowing and scraping. On the stairs I ask him if he'll take me out to practice driving.

"Certainly, m'lady," he says, winking at me. "At your service."

He gets right to work painting Room 3, and right on cue, starts whistling, "Whistle while you work."

Nick and I have just finished taping up the baseboards in the hallway, when TJ comes tromping up the stairs, swinging two cans of unopened "eggshell white" for the hall. A grimy surgeon's mask hangs from a cord around his neck. His green flannel shirt looks so soft. He sets the cans down and asks us if we've seen Mr. Creep lately.

Yay! You care! I love you!

Can't say that, so I tell him—Nick and I tell him, sitting cross-legged in the hall, TJ crouched down beside us—about Mr. Creep showing up in my Frost Fair photo, and how we spotted Mr. Creep and Bony the night of the ghost tour, and that we are stumped about what to do next, but that we know we have to do something.

"Probably ran off to south Florida with all the other nut jobs," TJ says. "That wife is scary-looking."

TJ really wants to talk to us! To me! Or maybe he just wants a break from scraping the stinky adhesive off the kitchen floor.

That's when Dad pops out of Room 3 and asks us to tell him more about Mr. Creep, which we do. All three of us do, while he leans against the wall, tugging on the bandana around his neck. I wonder at first if he's trying to avoid work, but I stop thinking that pretty quick as he listens to us tell everything we know about Mr. Creep. His mouth gets tighter and tighter and he shakes his head in disgust.

When we finish talking, he spits out, "That scum." Then he says, "He won't get away with it. We're gonna find that bastard." This isn't part of his act. He turns and stalks back to Room 3 like Mr. Creep's waiting in there for Dad to knock him senseless.

Well, this is weird. What's got him so worked up? I've never ever seen him flip out like this. I was hoping TJ would help us. But Dad? Wow.

TJ gives us thumbs up and heads back downstairs.

Nick and I high five, but I'm a little worried about Dad's anger. What's he going to do with it? Where's this going to lead us?

Chapter 13

NICK

The pirate hostel smells like pancakes and old clothes. It is a backpackers' hostel, where you stay overnight if you cannot afford Sha-Na-Na or even the Comfort Inn. To live there Taylor has worked out an arrangement with the owner. He gets a discount for helping around the place. He has to sleep in a room with bunk beds and other guys. Like a sleepover. I can imagine Kat saying that he is way too old to live at the hostel. I peek into a lounge on the first floor where The Black Eyed Peas play from an iPod dock. A girl with a pierced lip checks her email and two guys with kerchiefs over their long curly hair study a map of South America. They don't seem much older than Luna and me. I have a map collection that no one knows about—in a shoebox. Someday I want to be a traveler with a backpack. It's never occurred to me before. It's like I'm peeping through a keyhole to a fantastic world.

It might happen—if Kat will ever let me off being grounded for what we are about to do.

I'm freaked out.

Dad and Kat have gone to Jacksonville to pick up a load of tile. They have to get there before the store closes for the holiday.

Dad told us privately that he might take Kat out for fish tacos, to cheer her up. Kat told us privately not to go anywhere while they are away. She said we could order a pizza after we finished taping the edges of all the upstairs baseboards with blue painter's tape. But we were not to leave the house. "You're not to leave the house," she said three times. Luna finally said, "We heard you the first time," and Kat said, "Don't get smart with me."

As soon as Dad and Kat pulled out of the driveway, we dropped our rolls of tape and went to find Taylor. He was in the kitchen, wolfing down a slice of Kat's famous Godiva Chocolate Raspberry cake. With his hands. "While the cat's away," he said. He had white frosting in his whiskers. He looked happy. Wiping the crumbs on his jeans, he meowed. Luna rolled her eyes and, like a P.E. teacher, she said, "Let's hustle."

So we are at the pirate hostel to get his jacket and his car. The wind's picking up. A storm is expected. I keep thinking of *The Wizard of Oz* and Dorothy being lost and that gets all mixed up with Bony and Mr. Creep, and my heart is tap-dancing in my chest. Am I doing the right thing? I'm sick of the back and forth in my mind. I know not to let on. *Face your fear.* Finally an adult is paying attention to us. So many parents are all about their sexy hair and their cocktails and their yoga classes and their house remodels that they wouldn't know evil if it bit them on the ass. Like those girls and their Twitter feeds. If they slam me their parents won't even know. Or care.

We go out the back door of the hostel and get into Taylor's old Rambler. Luna sits in front and props her feet on the dashboard. She has her camera out. The last two days she has decided to wear only one earring, like her dad. A dangly silver half-moon. She and Taylor look like they belong together. They both have brown hair with natural fiery red glimmers. Of course, Luna has that copper wave that magically appeared last night. I sit in the back.

"You sure you know how to get there?" Taylor says.

We make eye contact in the rearview mirror. His eyes are brown and friendly. "Of course," I say. Then: "Seatbelts." Just like Kat—why do I sound like her?

We all latch our seatbelts. I want to say, "Why are you helping us?" As if he can read my mind, Taylor says, almost under his breath, "I can't stand guys like that."

We do not listen to music. The wind bats the car around on Manatee Bridge. New Year's Eve and there are plenty of people in town, all of them hoping for sunshine, no doubt, but—surprise!— the water and the sky and the sand and the trees all have a grayish look. Ten minutes later we turn into the subdivision across from the amphitheater. The amphitheater looks abandoned. I try to picture the Frost Fair, but those memories are almost erased. Now that we're almost there all I can think about is Bony, sitting across from Mr. Creep on that restaurant balcony, trying to seem grown-up. It's like he wanted her to be his *date* or something.

Taylor says, "Now, I've got a plan."

Luna says, "And that would be?" She sounds a little worried.

Taylor says, "Tell me when we're getting close. I want to park at least five houses away."

"You're getting close, " I say.

Luna says, "That's it."

We drive past the house and I count off five more. Taylor finds a little side street and parks the Rambler facing in the direction of a quick getaway. The silence when he cuts the engine is momentous— like a trumpet call. Life will never be the same after this. Somehow that's clear to me. I don't know why. I just know.

Taylor takes his tool belt out of the trunk and fastens it around his hips. He pulls a Miami Heat cap down snug on his head.

"Give me one of your phones," he says. I hand over my precious new phone. He cruises through the numbers to make sure Luna's number's in there. There aren't many numbers. Nana Fanny. Kat and Dad. Luna. Maeve. Caroline Rex. And another girl at school who called me one time. I'm embarrassed for him to see that I don't have many friends.

Sounding bossy, Taylor says, "I'm gonna go to a couple front doors and offer to do handyman work. So it'll just look like I need work. Maybe Mr. Creep'll hire me to do some little job. I'll tell him I saw some shingles flying off his roof. I'll get in that way. If I want you, I'll call you. Otherwise, don't leave the car."

He carries a small toolbox, like a doctor in a movie making a house call in olden times. We watch him walk away. He looks determined, leaning into the wind. It starts to rain. I'm skeptical. What kidnapper would care about house repairs? Or do all adults, even criminals, care about house repairs? And how will Taylor collect evidence from up on the roof?

I say, "What if he doesn't come back?"

Luna says, "Mom says that he used to just disappear." Then: "But this time I could drive us home." She fiddles with the keys he left in the ignition.

"Disappear? Like a ghost?"

"No, baby. Not like a *ghost.*"

"Like how?"

"Like a dad who doesn't want to be a dad."

"He doesn't seem that way now," I say.

"You've had an easy life, you know that?"

Tears pop into my eyes. "What're you talking about? My mom died."

No one says anything. We are parked under trees and the limbs whip around in the wind. A stupid time to be doing house repairs. Rain pelts the windshield.

I grit my teeth. I know Louise would say not to use the word *always,* but I want to say, "You always hurt my feelings."

Luna does not turn around. My face is hot with hate.

Finally I say, "This is the last time I'll do anything with you. Ever."

"I thought we were in this together." Her phone rings—some stupid song. "What happened?" she says.

There is a pause. Then she says, "We're coming!"

"What the hell?" I say.

But Luna is already out of the car, slinging her camera strap around her neck. We are going to get soaked. I get out and face the rain. We trudge toward Bony's house.

"I'm sorry," Luna says. "Okay?"

"I don't care," I say. "What's going on?" *This* will save me from those girls at school? Luna and her bright ideas.

"They're not there. He wants me to take pictures."

"Big trouble," I say. *Don't leave the house, don't leave the house, don't leave the house.* I have seen Kat irritated and mad. But I dread what she might do if we get caught. Deep in my heart, I realize that she will be worried about us. It is something we have in common—worry.

The neighborhood looks abandoned, except for a mother at one house dashing out in the rain to haul a bike into the garage. She does not notice us.

At the edge of Mr. Creep's lawn, Luna stops. She is so much taller than me. She has breasts. She has confidence. She puts one hand on my arm and says, "Hey. I mean it. I'm sorry." It's like she wants to clear the air before we face the consequences of snooping in Mr. Creep's house. She wants to be on the same team.

I count to five and then I say, "Okay." Our eyes meet for just a second, a flicker.

"Now let's get to work!"

We go up to the back door, as Taylor has instructed her. The red truck is nowhere around. The back door's open and we step into the kitchen. I imagine Mr. Creep jumping out from behind a curtain or a door.

Taylor comes down the hall.

Luna says, "How'd you get in here?"

Taylor winks and says, "An old trick." He waves a plastic library card. "I jimmied it open with this. Piece of cake." I file that away. Later I'll ask him to show me how.

I say, "So he might come back any minute?"

"He might," Taylor says. "We have to be quick."

Luna is already snapping photos, right and left.

Taylor says, "Come in here," and he leads us into the living room. It's a mess. The Christmas tree knocked over. Glass ornaments broken into shiny, sharp pieces. Clothes in piles. Magazines tossed around. And a plate of food rotted on the coffee table, like a science experiment. The Christmas tree makes me think that they pretended to be a real family.

Luna takes pictures. Finally Taylor says, "Give me the camera."

Luna says, "No way."

Taylor says, "Listen. There's stuff in the bedroom I don't want you to see."

Luna says, "The camera's my job!"

Taylor says, "Trust me. You have to trust me."

I imagine that Luna's thinking what I'm thinking: Why should we trust you? But she hands over her camera.

Taylor says, "Now, take a look in the bedroom, but don't *go* in."

We creep over to the bedroom doorway and peer in. There is a king size bed and beside the bed there is a dog crate, with a padlock. A crate for a very big dog. Inside the crate there is a comforter with surfer girls printed on it. And stuffed animals. Bony's clothes are folded in lumpy piles beside the crate. That cute bomber jacket and flannel pajama bottoms. Pink and white underpants. The closet door is open and men's clothing hangs there, pants and dress-up shirts. There is a neat row of polished shoes.

"Oh, my God," Luna says.

"Yeah," Taylor says. And: "All the other rooms are empty."

"He keeps her in the crate?" I say. It hasn't sunk in. My imagination hadn't gotten that far.

Luna just looks at me. This is worse than even she imagined.

Taylor says, "There's some stuff in here I don't want you to see. Magazines and shit. You wait at the window and let me know if you see them coming back. If they do, we'll skedaddle. Out the back door. And through the back yards—to the car."

"What if we get caught?" I say.

Taylor and Luna say, "Face your fear!"

We hide behind the curtains in the living room. I am trembling all over. I do not want to imagine the magazines. I do not want to imagine Bony crawling every night into a *crate*. But there it is: the evidence we crave. We listened to our intuition and this is where we ended up. The curtains smell smoky. And I feel that wetness, that little leak, my period starting. I can't wait to be back home. Facing fear isn't one of my top skills.

"My period's starting," I whisper and reach for Luna's hand and she tucks my hand inside hers. I'm glad I can tell her.

"Shit—we'll get home as soon as we can."

For some reason I remember last night when she asked me if I ever wished for a brother or sister. I'd always wished for a brother, but now I have a sister. Louise says you don't always get what you want. Be grateful. Vintage Louise.

We hear the truck before we see it. Then a flash of red through the leafless trees.

"They're coming!" Luna whispers loudly.

We meet Taylor at the kitchen door and the three of us leap out and run, with Taylor in the rear. He says, "Aim for that shed." When we get behind the shed in the next yard, he says, "Now go! That line of trees!" The ground is squishy from the rain. It's raining hard. We're soaked. He guides us from hiding spot to hiding spot, until we're back at the Rambler. Breathing hard, we sling open its doors and hop in. Taylor starts the engine in a flash. Rain pounds the car. A leak in the roof drips water onto me.

Luna and I sigh big.

Taylor says, "Cover up with that blanket." I find the fleece blanket on the floor and huddle under it. It smells linty and like doughnuts. He probably lives on doughnuts.

He drives in a slow, calm way, as if we have all the time in the world. Right past Mr. Creep's house. There sits the red pickup with the shotgun in the rear window.

Taylor says, "I have to keep the camera for a while."

Luna says, "That's my camera."

"I know that, kiddo. But it's my job to protect you."

Luna says, "What're you gonna do with the pictures?"

Taylor says, "I need to think."

"Think about what?"

Taylor catches my eye in the rearview mirror. His eyes flit from me to Luna. Finally he says, "I don't want to come in contact with the police." He sounds like "come in contact" means he might catch a deadly disease. "Just let me think about it."

I say, "It's our secret, right?"

Taylor and Luna say, "Yeah." Like we are making a sacred oath.

When we turn onto the highway and head back into town, Luna's phone rings. She holds it up like she wants to fling it out the window and never answer it.

"It's Mama," she says.

Taylor says, "Tough luck. You gotta answer."

"Hi, there," she says, trying to put a little bounce into it. She pushes the button for speakerphone.

Kat says, "Where *are* you?"

Luna says, "We . . . had to go out."

"Where's Taylor?"

"I don't know . . .for sure."

"You girls are *grounded.* You hear me? Grounded."

"For how long?" Luna says.

"That's for me to know and you to find out!"

"Mama!"

"Don't 'Mama' me! I'm going to send Jimmy to pick you up."

"Don't do that! We're not far!"

"There's a tornado watch. A tornado watch! Wherever you are, get back immediately."

And Kat does not even say goodbye.

Taylor says, "Oh, boy—"

I say, "Where's *my* phone?"

Taylor is driving and patting his pockets. "I don't know," he says. "I don't know where your phone is."

"That's my new phone!"

I picture it in the kitchen of Mr. Creep's house. I try not to imagine Mr. Creep finding my phone. What if he calls the numbers? He could call Luna and torment us. He could torment Maeve Murphy and her parents might call the police and I'd *never* have friends.

What then?

Chapter 14

LUNA

Dad lets us out of his Rambler a few blocks from the Sha, causing us to have to walk home through the storm. "It'll be worse if I'm with you," Dad says when he makes us get out of the car.

"Right," I tell him. "Worse for you."

"See you real soon," he says, and speeds off, splashing us as he goes.

The walk home is so wet and miserable and scary, due to the wind gusting the leaves and twigs and grit into our faces, plus the weird yellow sky and distant siren combo, that Nick and I don't get it together to come up with an alibi.

We burst through the back door of the Sha-Na-Na and stop in the mudroom to hang up our sopping wet jackets and tug off our soggy sneakers.

Mama and Jimmy can't wait. They crowd into the mudroom, asking what the hell we thought we were doing.

To stall for time, I kick my soggy sneakers under the bench. I decide to act all put out myself. "You *know* I'm supposed to do a portfolio about how I spent my Christmas vacation, and I had to get some more pictures."

Jimmy is still wearing his yellow rain slicker and his baseball cap with the pirate flag. "In the rain?"

"After we told you not to go anywhere?" With a shaking hand, Mama pushes wet strands of hair away from her face. Drops of rainwater slide down her pale cheek. Is it good for a pregnant woman to be out in the rain? What if we cause her to have a miscarriage? I don't want that. I'm scared about a baby, but I don't want that.

They stand in front of us, Mama with her arms folded, an inch taller than Jimmy, barring our way into the kitchen, where cardboard boxes of the Italian tile they just purchased are stacked against the new cabinets. For a second I feel bad, because they'd been so excited about bringing home that tile from Jacksonville, and now this. I've never deliberately disobeyed Mama before. I consider telling her the truth, but that would mean getting Dad in even more trouble than he's already in.

Nick must have the same thought. She says, "Luna wanted to get pictures of the rain. On the fort."

"So why'd *you* go, young lady?" Jimmy asks her. He's uncomfortable with all this confrontation. Nobody likes it, but sometimes you can get into the spirit of a good fight, or at least some people can, but he isn't one of them. He's acting like a father in an old black and white movie, speaking his lines. *Cheaper by the Dozen.* I start giggling.

"This is not funny," Mama says. She'd been worried, now she's mad. "There's a *tornado warning.*"

"You just said it was a *watch.*" I push past Mama and Jimmy into the kitchen where the pale, newly laid bamboo floor feels smooth under my damp socks and smells almost sweet. But the newly installed track lights make me feel like I'm under interrogation. I just want to take a bath. "I asked Nick to come with me, to help me," I say. "It's my fault."

Nick, still in the mudroom, groans. "Can we please just go change our clothes?"

Jimmy ignores her and fixes me with a disbelieving look. "Where's your camera?"

I always carry my camera in a tiny Vera Bradley backpack I got as a birthday present from Renda. But Dad still has my backpack and my camera! How'd I let that happen?

"Yeah, where is it?" Mama chimes in.

"Uh, I don't know."

"You *lost* it?" Mama says, bristling up like a cat.

I shrug. Should I pretend to panic? My feet are feeling colder by the second.

"Just great," Mama says, raising her voice. "You'll have to buy a new one with your own money."

"Fine," I yell.

"Nick," Jimmy says. "Where's your phone? I kept trying to call you."

"I guess I dropped it," Nick says. "Sorry. Sorry I'm not perfect!"

"Where?" Jimmy says.

"Don't know."

"You'd better go back and look for it!" Jimmy says, now mad for real.

"Right now?" Mama turns on Jimmy. "In the rain?"

He waves Mama's question aside. "Okay, so it's gone. Ya'll lost a camera and a phone in one day. How'd you manage that?"

I really want to tell them the truth, about the cage with the pink comforter, about that awful house, about how brave Nick and I were, about how Dad cared enough to help us. But I know saying all this would only make things worse.

"What gave you the idea we're made of money?" Mama says.

"We didn't do it on purpose," Nick spits out, red-faced, at Mama, like she hates her.

"That doesn't matter." Mama glares at Nick. I know she doesn't hate Nick. She hates being sassed. But I'm hating all this hating and I feel like weeping.

"To your rooms," Jimmy says, pointing.

"I'll call the fort, I'll call the fort," I say. "They must have a lost and found."

Behind his back, Nick makes chopping motions with her hands, à la Rosemary and Polly, which makes me feel better for two seconds.

That night at dinner, they inform us, speaking as a united front, that we are grounded, except for necessary errands, until school starts. We will help them get the Sha ready. No discussion.

Nick and I exchange glum looks over our pasta. How will we rescue Bony if we can't leave the house? I know she's worried about her phone, hoping that Mr. Creep didn't find it. Worried that he might come after us. We need to find Dad and gather our evidence and go to the police.

"What about New Year's Eve?" I ask. "I got invited to a party." Bethany's. I wouldn't have gone anyway, but they don't need to know that.

"Me too," Nick says, and I don't know if she has, but God bless her for saying so. "How're we ever supposed to make new friends? Can't you make an exception for New Year's frickin Eve?"

Mama frowns. She can usually be persuaded to change her mind.

Jimmy takes her hand. At least they still love each other, baby and all. "Sorry," he says. "No exceptions. Grounded is grounded."

Later that night, after the storm blows over, needing some fresh air, I slip on my down jacket and go outside to sit on the damp front porch steps. It's cold and dark, no stars, which suits my mood. At a house down the street, snatches of laughter and Glenn Miller swell up whenever someone opens the front door. I miss playing in a band. I only hurt myself by not trying out for band here.

Why do I always realize things too late?

A few blocks away, a police siren pulses. Is Bony already shut in her cage for the evening? I'll be haunted forever by the sight of that cage, that pink comforter, that big stuffed rabbit with the buck teeth. A car rolls down our street, the lone driver rubbernecking at house numbers.

I jump up, deciding to head back inside and Facebook message Renda about the latest developments, but Molly's Honda Accord wheels into the driveway next door. Someone I can talk to!

Molly climbs out of her car and saunters over in my direction, dressed only in a tank top and sweatpants, holding a Publix grocery bag on her hip, blabbing as she walks toward me about the fabulous New Year's Eve party she's going to tomorrow. When she stops to take a breath I blurt out the whole story about going to Mr. Creep and Bony's house, and the cage, and that my dad now has my camera and that we need to go show the evidence we've gotten to the police but I'm not sure where my dad is or what he plans to do with the evidence. "We've got to *do* something to help that kid."

Molly wigs out like I've never seen her, wide-eyed and gasping, clutching her bag of groceries to her chest. "My God. A cage, really? That *poor girl*. I see them all the time! They come to the Alligator Farm every day at noon. For our show. Him and her. *Every single day*. It's so weird. We should kidnap her back from him!"

I tell her that he knows who Nick and I are and that he's suspicious of us and we can't let him see us. And he might have Nick's phone! I don't mention the fact that we're grounded.

Molly suggests we come to the Alligator Farm the day after New Year's when she's working and she'll show us where to hide. "He always leaves her sitting on a bench after the show to go and get her some popcorn. It's like a ritual they have."

"We'll grab her then."

"Come the day after New Year's. That's the next time I work." Molly heads back to her place.

That's a long time away, but it seems like our best option at the moment. I stand there watching her go, thinking mixed up thoughts about being grounded unfairly and not knowing where my dad or my camera or Nick's phone is and that stuffed rabbit and Mama and Jimmy refusing to believe that Bony is in danger, and Mama keeping the baby a secret and Rosemary and Polly, who took things into their own hands.

Nick and I are going to get Bony, or whatever her real name is, away from that monster. If none of the adults help, we'll do it ourselves.

Mama and Jimmy aren't grounded, so they get to go out and celebrate New Year's Eve. That afternoon, Jimmy strolls in just as Nick and I finish painting the last guest room. Teal green—"Aquaduct." Nick and I picked out the color. They aren't going out because they *want* to, Jimmy tells us. It's a Chamber of Commerce party.

They'll be home right after midnight. Nana Fanny will be coming over to *hang out* with us. Not as a babysitter, just to keep us company. They'd *much* rather stay home with us and play Scrabble, but this is something they have to do for their business. Meet the local movers and shakers, and so on.

While he's still talking, I walk out and back to my room.

Mama and I have always spent New Year's Eve together. It's our tradition. Some years it was just the two of us and we watched sappy movies or *Gilmore Girls* and baked chocolate chip cookies and waved sparklers. A couple years I had slumber parties and Mama read everyone's tarot cards. In New Mexico we had a campfire beside the Rio Grande. At Alligator Point we invited neighbors over, everyone dressed up in crazy costumes and we ran around on the beach banging on pots and pans. When Mama was married to Brad, in Tallahassee, they had grown up dinner parties and I got to invite a few of my friends, too.

But now, evidently all that is over, to hell with tradition, and Mama sent Jimmy in to tell me. Fine, if that's how she wants it. I will welcome Nana Fanny with open arms. Bring it on.

Nana Fanny arrives around nine, parking her VW bug about a foot from the curb. In her quilted shopping bag: two bottles of non-alcoholic Champagne, three silver party hats that say *Happy New Year!*, a Tupperware container full of homemade Chex mix, chocolate bars with dried cherries and walnuts in them.

Of course she's all dolled up in a gold tunic and leggings. Sparkly chandelier earrings and musky patchoulish perfume. I squeal and hug her thin shoulders, overdoing it. I love her, so I *am* glad to see her, but Mama and Jimmy, all dressed in black party clothes, are standing there, and so is Nick, wearing PJs, just like me, and I'm not going to let on how disappointed I am that Mama is ditching me.

I let Mama kiss my cheek, but I don't kiss her back. "Happy New Year, Pumpkin," she says. "I'll be thinking of you at midnight!"

Right.

After the traitors are gone, Nana, Nick and I launch into party mode. None of us wants to sulk or be serious. We play Hearts and Crazy Eights. We make popcorn and eat it with Nana's chocolate and Chex Mix. We get out the Twister game, and Nana, because she does yoga three mornings a week, is always the last one standing and wins every round, her face flushed and her earrings swinging all over the place. We play 1960s soul music on Jimmy's dining room iPod—Aretha Franklin and Sam Cooke—and Nick and I kick off our slippers and Nana kicks off her flats and we dance like maniacs, slipping and sliding on the shiny refinished floor. Nick's pajama pants keep falling down, which cracks us up.

When we've worn ourselves out, sacked out on the new furniture in the Florida room, Nana Fanny asks if we want her to read to us, which doesn't sound babyish, but just right. I bring down *The Secret of the Old Clock*, which she reads aloud in a silly, dramatic voice.

It's then that my mind starts to wander. What are Mama and Jimmy doing right now? 11:30 on New Year's Eve. I hope they are having a terrible, awful time. I hope she's not drinking. And Renda? At a party, making out with a cute guy. Which leads me to TJ. I don't have a clue where he is, but I wish wish wish he and I were on the beach, alone, nestled under a blanket beneath the stars. I let out a groan and change the mental channel. Dad? I hope he's not getting into trouble with the pirates. I've got to get my camera! Bony. I want to run out and find her. Can we really wait until the day after tomorrow at the Alligator Farm?

Nana, swallowed up in the big, overstuffed armchair, gold sequins on her top glimmering, finishes the chapter, shuts the book, and drops it in her lap. "The witching hour is almost nigh. You wanna hear what we did when I lived on the cruise ship? To celebrate New Year's?"

"The SS Aurora," Nick says dreamily. She's lying with her head at the other end of the couch, and she keeps tapping me with her pink painted toes.

I've never heard anything about Nana's life on the cruise ship. Jimmy doesn't like to talk about it. "Tell us," I say.

"We'd be down in the Caribbean somewhere, and the air would be soft, you know what I mean? Warm, too, but we'd have a fire in the fireplace just because. And a big dinner and dance. Everyone who wanted to, officers and crew and musicians and guests, near midnight, we'd sit down and make a list of the things we'd done that year that we wanted to put behind us. Things we regretted, things we didn't want to dwell on or take into the New Year with us. Then at the stroke of midnight we'd toss our lists into the fireplace and shout, "To Will Pekins!" and raise our glasses and toast the New Year. So liberating!" She cackled. "What we did after that I'd rather not say. Something we could write about on next year's list."

"Will Pekins?" I ask. "Who's that?"

"I got no idea," she says. "Maybe the guy who started the

tradition? It was just something we said."

"A fireplace on a boat," Nick says. Sleepy.

"Let's do that now," I say, sitting up. "Let's make lists."

"Let's do," Nana says.

"I'll get the pens and paper," Nick says, and she's wide awake and on her feet.

Nana finishes her list first and folds her paper into a little square, saying she doesn't do nearly enough wicked things anymore. She disappears into the living room to start the fire.

Nick and I both have long lists, which we don't let each other see. I can guess what she writes. You can guess what I write. But at the bottom of my list, in all caps, underlined, I write FEELING SORRY FOR MYSELF. That one surprises me. But it's true.

In the living room, Nana has the fake Champagne poured into thin little glasses and has set them on a table beside the roaring, crackling fire, which smells like the cedar log Jimmy placed on top of the kindling. Smiling at each other, we put on our pointy silver hats and stand with our folded paper, ready to do the deed. When the grandfather clock in the hall strikes twelve, and the world outside explodes with firecrackers and fireworks and honking, we toss our papers into the flames and shout "To Will Pekins!" Then we stand there and watch last year's mistakes turn black. Nana's right. It is liberating.

We raise our chilly glasses and toast.

"Off with the old, in with the new!" Nana crows.

"Look out, 2010, here we come!" Nick says.

"To new traditions!" I say.

We settle down in armchairs around the fire, waiting for Mama and Jimmy to come home, not talking much, and I guess I drowse off.

I wake to Nana yelling, "Oh my God. The chimney's on fire!"

Chapter 15

Nick

Chaos and bedlam! Gray smoke billows from the chimney! From all over the B, six smoke alarms are chattering away like cyborgs: Warning! Evacuate immediately! We all shriek like a herd of mice has been let loose. Nana dials 911 and Luna darts helter-skelter out of the house, shouting, "Shit! Shit! Shit! I need my camera!" I take the stairs faster than ever. I grab my mother's wooden box, hug it to my chest with one arm, and slide down the banister, landing at the front door. Nana's there, a barefooted banshee, waving at me wildly, shouting, "Get out, get out, get out!" Sirens clanging, a fire truck plods into our front yard and four firefighters leap toward the B. The smoke is black and soupy now, flowing out the front door.

I huddle with Nana for a minute but cast around for Luna. If our house burns down, it'll be on TV, and maybe all those girls will feel sorry for me and not torment me when school starts. Selfish, selfish, selfish. Maybe this will do: the something extraordinary, the headline Luna says I need. She and TJ are sitting a few houses away on the hood of his car—where'd he come from? A mercury streetlight shines on them like a spilled Orange Crush. How'd TJ know about it so fast? He has his arm around Luna. Neighbors—most of them in PJs and robes—stand on their porches. Dad's going to be furious. I set my mother's box between my shoes. I don't want to lose touch with it.

And there Dad is, alarm all over his face. Dad and Kat rush us, arms open. Dad pulls me close. He smells like fried food and wine. Here are the first words out of his mouth: "Are you all right?" Me. It's me he's worried about. Kat wanders over to Luna and TJ. Dad holds me tight and makes room for Nana with his other arm.

"I'm so sorry, Jimmy," Nana says.

Dad says, "Here, take my shoes." And he slips out of his loafers and Nana slips into them. She's clutching her purse.

"This will set you back," Nana says.

"That's not important," Dad says. "You're safe. That's what's important." He's saying this to *me*.

There never is any fire—genuine flames, searing heat. It's all smoke damage. After about a half hour, it's all over. The whole time I am standing here holding my dad's hand. It's warm. He doesn't seem worried. Nana heads for her car, singing some old song with "New Year's Eve" in the lyrics. Kat has been sitting on TJ's hood all this time. The fire chief chats with Dad and then waves good night. In his stocking feet, Dad goes up and locks the front door. He pokes his feet into work boots that he always leaves on the porch. I pick up my mother's wooden box. Kat and Luna come over to see what's going on. They look so much alike, long legs, brown shiny hair, cute pointy chins. I am vaguely aware of TJ's Nova grinding away and people drifting back into their houses. It's way after midnight.

"Gals," Dad says, "We are going to a motel."

Kat says, "Are you serious?"

"Kid, you can't go in there yet," and he says that straight to her, as if he means *only her*. "But first, how about some Spudnuts?"

Luna speaks up finally, wistfully: "We haven't been there in ages." She's probably thinking about TJ. I know I would be.

Spudnuts was a 1940s chain of doughnut shops. They went out of business, but a few shops kept the name. In Coquina Bay they are open 24/7. "Yeah. Spudnuts," I say.

In the car Luna says, "What about the Sha? Don't you feel bad?"

Dad says, "Horrible."

There's a rustle in the dark front seat, like maybe Dad's reaching for Kat's hand.

Dad says, "We need to gear down."

Kat says, "Rome wasn't built in a day." And: "I am *so* sleepy."

Spudnuts is out on the highway. There's a blinking blue sign in the window. Inside it's warm and cozy. Stuff from the 1940s covers the walls. Pictures of guys in military uniforms. Pin-up girls. Paintings of milkmen delivering milk to houses. We take a booth and Dad goes up to order. Each booth has its own jukebox and I ask Kat for fifty cents and play "Boogie-Woogie Bugle Boy." Dad brings back a tray of warm Spudnuts, coffee for him, and hot chocolates for Kat, me, and Luna. Luna and I sit on one side, Dad and Kat on the other. It feels like we're having a meeting.

And it turns out we are.

Dad says, "We've got something to tell you."

Luna and I glance sideways at each other. I think we both wonder if we're in more trouble, mega-trouble. Luna has powdered sugar all around her mouth.

Kat says, "Nothing like hot grease and sugar to cap off a fine evening."

Dad says, "Darlin'."

Kat says, "Well, we're all waiting." She's grinning.

Dad says, "This is good news. Very good news. I'm thrilled about it."

I am thinking maybe we're going to move back to Tallahassee.

Dad claps his hands together and says, "We…are going to have a baby!"

Luna rears back dramatically. "A baby? Like a real baby? Like the kind that cry and vomit?"

I am speechless.

Kat says, "That kind—yes. But also cute, we hope."

"Like you gals," Dad says. He looks right at me. He says, "You'll be a big sister."

He's waiting for me to say something. They all are. I am thinking *so they still do it* and *I will be in college when this baby is in kindergarten* and *what if it's a boy* and *what about the ambience of the B*? If they can have a baby, I want a puppy. In your dreams, sweetheart, I imagine Dad saying.

Luna has her phone out. She's scrolling through her photos of the fire. I am so jealous. I want my new phone. I want my own little world. I sip my hot chocolate. It burns my tongue, but I don't say anything. Dad and Kat act nonchalant, but they are waiting. For me.

Dad says, "Hey, we're a family. Our family's expanding."

I smile at him. "I'll be a big sister," I say.

And Dad sighs, relieved. He reaches out for my hand. I bat him away.

I store all this up to tell Louise. Our house caught fire, we're having a baby, I was humiliated at the sleepover, Luna's dad tried to help us, I lost my phone, I've become a big time liar, and we did not make any progress helping Bony. Life is coming at me faster than I can get it under control. I used to think that if I got good grades, everything was under control. That was before my mom died.

Out the big window—beside our booth—neon lights crash up against each other, lots of color. Like a rainbow in curlicues. Almost too much to see clearly. But there is no missing the red pickup that pulls into the parking lot. And Mr. Creep gets out, glances around suspiciously, hitches up his slacks, locks his truck, and makes a beeline for the front door of Spudnuts.

"Let's play some more songs," I say. Dad spins quarters on the table and we all try to be in charge of the jukebox. Kat always says, "Thank the goddesses," and Nana Fanny always says, "Thank the Lord" in that southern way she has. I don't know who to thank, but I *am* thankful I'm with my family. I feel protected.

Chapter 16

LUNA

I can't tell how Nick really feels about a new baby, but she definitely doesn't freak out. She has a little smile on her face, but she's twisting up a straw and untwisting it and twisting it again. Mama and Jimmy are watching her, trying to read her mind.

I'm surprised that Jimmy just spilled the beans, right there under the bright lights in the crowded Spudnuts, especially after he and Mama came home to fire trucks and then had to face up to the fact that we'll have to fork over more money to repair the chimney and clean up the smoke damage and that the Sha may not open on time. Jimmy doesn't seem to be upset or mad about any of it. Instead he's acting all happy and aren't we lucky?

It's Mama's turn to pick a song on the jukebox so she plays Elvis singing "Blue Moon," with that weird clip-clopping background noise, not exactly a Happy New Year kind of song.

I'm sliding through the pics on my phone and my favorite is the one of TJ sitting on the hood of his car, elbows on his knees, smiling with half-closed eyes. So weird how he just happened to be driving past right when the fire trucks arrived and the air was full of smoke. He parked and I went over to sit with him on his car hood to watch the firemen striding around and the neighbors huddling and pointing. TJ smelled like booze, but I didn't care, I just scooted over next to him and started to cry a little, just nerves—we all made it out all right and the Sha was still standing. He tucked me under his arm and he felt so warm and I snuggled close. Then he took my hand and held it. *Held my hand!* And started telling me about some wild party he'd been to down at the beach, skinny dipping, blah blah blah, and that he'd just taken his girlfriend Jillian home, and he was headed to another party south of town—some guy was having a bonfire. He didn't say anything romantic, but I wasn't really listening anyway, because he was *holding my hand*, probably because he felt sorry for me, but who cares, he kept holding it until the trucks left and Mama came over to tell me it was okay to come back inside. I wish he'd asked me to go with him, not that Mama would've let me go, but if he'd only asked me, life would be perfect. And if he hadn't mentioned his girlfriend.

So I'm just sitting there in the booth in Spudnuts, eating one glazed donut after another, thinking about TJ and hoping he got to the party okay and wondering what *our* baby would look like if we had one—stupid thoughts like that—when Mr. Creep comes sidling in the Spudnuts door like a creature from a nightmare. This guy—every time we turn around. At least Bony's not with him. I reach over and sink my claws into Nick's thigh and she lets out a little squeal.

I'm praying, *Please don't let him see us.* But he swivels his head, casing out the room. He catches sight of us and keeps looking and I can't help but stare back. He looks so ordinary. He doesn't *look* evil, not right now. He doesn't even look scary. He's not the kind of guy you'd ever notice. Tall but kind of hump-shouldered, wearing horn-rimmed glasses I've never seen him wear. His ponytail is gone and he now has regular old guy hair. He keeps staring at us like he's deciding what to do. Does he have Nick's phone? Will he come over and return it? Or mention it? That wouldn't be good.

In my head I'm saying, *leave, leave or at least ignore us*, but no. He abandons his place in line, strolls straight toward our table.

Oh, God. He stops right in front of us.

I'm mesmerized by the sleeve of his shiny black leather jacket. I can't look him in the face.

He thrusts out his big hand toward Jimmy and Mama and says, "Hi, I'm Mason Jacobson. I recognized your girls here." So not his real name!

Then to Nick and me, in a jolly voice, "Just wanted to check and see if you ever found that dog's home!"

Mama dabs her mouth with a napkin and says, "What dog?"

"Oh, yeah. " I force my gaze upward. "We did!"

His mouth is smiling, but his eyes, behind the glasses, are like a weapon.

I say, "Uh. That was TJ's dog."

Jimmy frowns. "What were you doing with TJ's dog?"

Nick says, "He ran off and we found him. We didn't know he was TJ's dog at first."

"*What* now?" says Mama.

Mr. Creep chuckles and his belly shakes. "Oh, it wasn't no big deal. Didn't mean to get your girls in trouble! They knocked on our door, right before Christmas, to see if the dog they found was our dog. It wasn't, but we sure did want to keep him. Cute little thing. Terrier, wasn't it? We just love dogs. We got a dog at home and we miss him. Me and the wife and the grandkids."

Does he know we've seen his dog crate? And why does he keep mentioning a wife and grandkids?

"What kind of dog do you have, Mr. Jacobson?" Nick asks in a chipper voice. Is she thinking about the dog crate, too?

"She's a collie mix," Mr. Creep says, and gives her an insincere smile. His top incisor overlaps. He doesn't care about dogs, or people.

Silence, except for Elvis crooning. My elbow slips on the

greasy tabletop. An entire family of blondes burst through the door, causing a hubbub with their laughing and jostling.

Jimmy sips his coffee.

Mama says, "Well, Happy New Year!"

"Same to you," says Mr. Creep. "Good to meet you! Hey, didn't catch your names."

Mama tells him! And mentions the Sha-Na-Na!

Now Nick is clawing my thigh.

"You all come stay with us next time you're in town," Jimmy says.

Nick and I don't say a word until Mr. Creep has left Spudnuts with his box of donuts. Then we tell Mama and Jimmy who they've just been speaking to.

To my surprise, they both laugh.

"You two," Mama says. "He's a nice man. You've been watching too much *Dateline*."

I say, "*Dateline's* got nothing to do with it!"

Jimmy says, "They'd find something sinister in a Cracker Jack box. Now let's get home and start the New Year in a better frame of mind."

We know a lot more than we can tell them, Nick and me, which is so frustrating. But we can't tell them, not yet, so we just stuff the last bits of donuts into our mouths and file out behind Jimmy.

New Year's Day. Wiping soot off the walls around the fireplace and cleaning the floors and window. Not a great way to start 2010.

Jimmy, on his hands and knees, stares up into the chimney, "Should've gotten this thing really scrubbed out before we used it. By somebody better than Sweeps R Us."

"Oh, now," Mama says, dreamily smearing newspaper on a window. "You can call someone tomorrow."

At least they're getting along.

All day I wait, stewing, hoping Dad will show up with my camera, but he never does. What if he's run off with it? It's got all my important photos on it. Evidence. Photos for my school project. I should never have let him take it. When will I learn? I promise myself I'll hunt him down and get it back. Even if he's left town I'll find him. I call the pirate hostel and they say that he's not there, but he hasn't checked out. So where the hell is he?

That night, at Nana Fanny's house, we have black-eyed peas and greens and cornbread and afterwards play Apples to Apples and Scrabble. Mama wins at Scrabble, like always. Then Jimmy tells Nana Fanny about the new baby and she squeals and gets up and hugs us all and sashays around the kitchen, singing "Baby baby baby, oh!" until we all laugh and join in.

The next morning, I beg beg beg Mama to let us go to the fort to look for the lost camera and lost phone. This is the day she and Jimmy plan to lay the new kitchen backsplash, but right now Jimmy is busy making calls about the chimney, and I know that, even though we're grounded, I can work her.

She finally says okay but we have to make it quick. Ride to the fort, hopefully find the gadgets and be back in an hour and a half to pitch in.

Late morning, Nick and I set off, peddling our bikes madly, but not towards the fort. The day is splendidly warm and sunny. Even though we're going on a scary mission, and I'm worried about the fate of my camera, it's sweet to be free of the Sha. The sun feels so good through my sweatshirt that I want to jump off my bike and lie down on the brown grass beside the road and soak up it up. But there's no time for that. We have a strict schedule.

I ride in front and my backpack keeps me from seeing Nick over my shoulder, but I hear her tires spraying up rocks behind me. Trucks rumble and cars whiz past, some with loud tunes playing, people headed for the beach. The nice weather does not go along with our dark mission. We have lied to Mama again. We are already in trouble and are about to get into more.

"Hurry hurry hurry," Nick keeps chanting.

I want to tell her to shut up, but don't waste the energy. Up ahead are the white concrete walls of the Alligator Farm. Inside, Molly's waiting for us. And we have to get there and hide before Bony and Mr. Creep are due to arrive.

In my jeans pocket, my cell phone rumbles, but I ignore it and then turn it off, even though I know it must be Mama. She cancelled Nick's phone service, but Mr. Creep, if he does have Nick's phone, would've already gotten all the information he can get from it. He could have seen Nick's phone log, and her text messages, and pictures, and…he knows our names and where we live, thanks to Jimmy. I can't think about it. But after today, Mr. Creep will never bother Bony, or anyone else, ever again.

We wheel into the parking lot of the Alligator Farm and cut over to a side entrance, employees only, where Molly is supposed to let us in. The parking lot's already full of minivans and SUVs, but, thank God, no red pickup truck. I text Molly and after a few minutes she opens the gate, wearing her safari hat and uniform, nervous. "I could get fired for this," she mutters. When I talked to her on the porch on New Year's Eve she'd been all tough and sure of herself. "Can't believe you talked me into this," she says. "Sure you want to do it?"

I say, "We rode all the way out here, didn't we?"

Nick looks bug-eyed but resolute, like she's gearing herself up to march inside a haunted house.

Our plan, one that we quickly work out with Molly, is that we'll hide in a temporarily empty bird exhibit which is close to the alligator pond in the middle of the park, right behind the bench where Creep and Bony usually take in the show. We'll wait in there for Creep and Bony to arrive, observe them as they watch the show for the hundredth time, and then when he goes for popcorn, bam, we'll make our move.

Molly sneaks us into the empty aviary and we scooch down behind some giant ferns right behind "their" bench. The cage stinks like bird poop, really bad, and the gravel beneath us is green with mold. Small white feathers are plastered to the wire sides of the cage. We kneel there watching the people milling about, waiting for the show. What if someone happens to see two girls crouched down in a bird cage? I'd giggle if I wasn't so scared.

"What kind of birds were in here?" Nick says in a low voice.

"How can you think about birds?" I snap at her. "White ones. I don't know."

"Maybe egrets."

"It's disgusting in here." I'm starting to get frightened. Maybe we are doing a really, really stupid thing. What if we're scooped up and added to Mr. Creep's menagerie? Nick and I are already in a cage, like Bony's. Is it too late to get the hell out of here? I feel a stab of panic. "What'll we do with her when we get her? What'll we do?" We haven't worked this part out yet.

"Here they are," Nick says. "They're coming. Oh crap."

The two of them emerge from the crowd, Bony wearing a short red dress and metallic sandals, trailing behind Mr. Creep, in his dark sunglasses, and, even though there are plenty of empty benches, Mr. Creep leads them to the one right in front of us, the one where, according to Molly, they always sit. The two of them plop down, and I'm reminded of the time Nick and I saw them at the movie theatre, how he put his arm around her and it didn't look right. It doesn't look right now, either. Bony, in her skimpy red dress, huddles on the opposite end of the bench from Mr. Creep, who has his arm slung over the back, his big hand dangling, so he can snatch her real quick.

I could grab his throat with both hands and squeeze.

Nick is breathing too loudly.

Molly starts the feeding, doing her patter about alligators, and all the while Mr. Creep delivers his own quiet speech to Bony. I can't hear what he's saying, but he keeps talking and talking and I know, from the tone of his voice, and from the way she stares down at the pavement, that he's threatening her in some way. How can she just sit there? I want to yell at her, Run! Run!

There are so many other people around. A group of wholesome teenagers wearing turquoise t-shirts that say "Christ is Cool." Families of sunburnt northerners. Shriveled up, leather-clad Harley couples. Somebody will help her. We'll help her!

But she just sits there, still and silent, looking almost bored while he mumbles.

Finally the show ends. Nick and I clutch hands. Mr. Creep stands up and unfolds himself, very deliberately. He reaches down and grabs Bony's chin and makes her look at him. Then he nods toward the Alligator pit. "They're still hungry, I bet," he says, and smiles, revealing those overlapped teeth. "So you stay put. I'll get you the jumbo size today."

As soon as he walks away, before I can chicken out, I reach out and tap Bony on her bare shoulder, hoping she won't scream or startle. She turns her head, looks us over and must recognize us, but she squinches up her face like she smells something bad. That's all! Doesn't ask us what we we're doing there, in a freaking birdcage!

"We're gonna help you," I say.

"Come back here, quick," Nick says. "We'll let you in the cage. You can hide with us."

"Hurry!" I say. "We'll get you back to your real parents."

She shakes her head. When she speaks I can barely hear her. She says, "He's all I got."

"No!" Nick says, too loud. "He's a bad man. "

Bony shakes her head again and speaks louder this time. "Ya'll crazy."

Nick turns up her palms, like, now what?

Finally, just when Mr. Creep is first in line at the counter to purchase the popcorn, his broad back still to us, Bony jumps up.

Oh shit, it's really going to happen.

But no. Bony gives us a smirk and struts away, right towards Mr. Creep, her arm outstretched for the popcorn she evidently wants more than her freedom.

Chapter 17

NICK

When Bony says, "He's all I got," a scream sits in my throat, dying to get out.

We wait in the cage with bird droppings and feathers all around. Plague City, no doubt. A bath is all I want, and my phone, of course. Every waking minute, I picture my phone, lost. Sometimes I picture nice messages from Maeve Murphy. Sometimes I picture not-so-nice Facebook updates about the spa sleepover. I have to pee real bad. Finally they stroll toward the snake house.

We get out of the cage. Into pale sunshine. The warmth feels good. We walk away like those ladies who walk at the mall, arms pumping, our backs to Bony. I have the urge to turn around, but I'm afraid Mr. Creep would stare at me and know what's in my heart. I grab Luna's hand and hiss, "Let's split!" We blur past the gift shop, out into the parking lot.

My hands are shaking hard, and my bike lock won't unlock. Crying is out of the question, but I have that tight lump in my throat that says, "Hide! You might cry!" I wish we'd come on our skateboards—that would have made for a quicker getaway. Maybe I shouldn't be so quick to get rid of that skateboard. (As if quick getaways will be a major concern for the rest of my life.) My shoes have bits of gray bird fluff and white bird poop all around the toes.

Cars swing into the parking lot and kids spill out of the cars. To everyone but us it's a holiday. Everyone but us and Bony.

Luna says, "There's Dad!"

Taylor pulls up in the Rambler, smooth and easy. He says, "I thought I'd find you here. Get in."

"What about our bikes?" I say.

"Later, alligator."

I'm thinking *first the iPhone, then the camera, now our bikes*, but we climb into Taylor's car, me in back, Luna in the front. She puts her feet up on the dash and says, "I thought you'd never get here!" They laugh hysterically. And I feel left out.

"Seatbelts," I say, and we latch in.

He takes the back way across the employee parking lot. Gravel flies from under the tires. Taylor catches my eye in the rearview mirror and grins. He has ditched his earring and shaved. He has on a clean white t-shirt under a sports coat that looks suspiciously like Dad's. It *is* Dad's—a linen jacket the color of Cheerios.

"What about my phone?"

Taylor says, "I hope we find it."

That's so lame. He lost my phone. He ought to say, "I'll get you a new phone," but it's clear that Taylor could never afford to replace my phone.

"Seriously," Luna says, "where're you taking us?"

"Let's play a game," Taylor says. "Close your eyes real tight. See if you can feel where we're headed with your eyes closed."

I barely close my eyes. Sunshine seems to bleed through my eyelids. "Did *you*?" I say to Luna, my hand on her shoulder.

"Yep."

And to Taylor I say, "They were there."

Taylor reaches back and pats my knee. I loosen my seatbelt as far as it will go—just like I weigh around three hundred pounds—and I scooch up and lay one hand on his shoulder and one hand on Luna's. We are all connected. We turn left twice and I open my eyes and shout, "Nana Fanny's!"

"Bingo!" Taylor says. "Well, almost. We're going to see Sherry-baby."

"Nick's got the bump of direction," Luna says. She sounds proud of me.

Taylor says, "And that will come in handy all your life."

Luna says, "Especially when we do this."

Very carefully, like he's afraid of getting a traffic ticket, Taylor parks in Sherry's driveway. He says, "So you're gonna make a habit of it?"

Luna says, "We just might."

We. Luna said *we* like she meant it.

Taylor checks himself out in the rearview mirror. He swipes his head as if he could straighten his hair, but he doesn't have much. Behind his back Kat has said, "Looks like T-Bone saw the jailhouse barber." I have to bite my tongue to keep from calling him T-Bone.

"How do I look?" he says to Luna.

"Like a grown-up," she says.

We get out of the car and go to the trunk where Taylor has stashed Luna's backpack and camera. He hands it over to her. Luna's face lights up. I'm guessing she thought she might never see that camera again. Sherry's police bike—a heavy-duty black mountain bike with impressive tire treads—leans on a kickstand in front of her house.

Taylor fidgets at the door, shifting from one foot to another. "I had to make up my mind," he says. "It's the right thing to do."

"You got that right," Luna says.

He takes a deep breath and rings the doorbell.

Sherry opens the door, like she's been waiting for us. She holds open the storm door and says, "Come in, come in." She's in uniform, black shorts that come down to her knees and a black shirt, all of it ironed into sharp creases. Her hair's pulled back into a no-nonsense ponytail. Her cop stuff is spread all over the coffee table. An orange flashlight, handcuffs, and a gun, a real gun in a holster. And a helmet. The gun looks heavy. She's going on bike duty and wears black mountain-biking shoes.

Taylor introduces himself again. Sherry looks amused. "We've met. Remember. And we talked on the phone."

He is trying real hard to be polite and normal. His hands with their homemade tats tremble a little bit.

Luna says, "So you told her?"

"I did," Taylor says.

"Let's see what you've got, " Sherry says.

Taylor says, "I need to censor the photos."

"Oh, yeah?" Sherry says.

"There're some the girls can't see."

Taylor sits down on the sofa beside Sherry. Luna and I sit on the loveseat, leaning toward them. They click through the photos.

Sherry says, "What's with all the body parts?"

Luna shrugs.

I say, "She's got a good eye—her art teacher says so."

"Mr. Fulton?" Sherry says. She concentrates hard on the photos, frowning.

Luna says, "Yeah, Mr. Fulton."

"I had him, too. I learned a lot from dear old Fulty."

"You call him Fulty?" Luna says.

"Don't you?" Sherry says. That's a tidbit Luna loves. I can picture her telling the other photography-geeks.

Then Sherry says, "Go back a couple." Then, "There, that one."

"Can we see?" Luna says.

Taylor waves us over. We scramble and stand behind them. It's Mr. Creep and Bony that first day at the Alligator Farm—a rare shot for Luna, almost a portrait.

Sherry says, "Look at that!"

Luna says, "What?"

"Zoom in—look at their ears!"

I can see it—their ears stick out in exactly the same way. Luna says, "Do you think he really is her dad?"

Sherry says, "Not necessarily. But I bet you they're related."

"Gross," I say.

Sherry says, "Did you think to get his license number?"

We groan. Taylor says, "No, but the truck's a Dodge Ram. From out of state."

"From where," Sherry says, flipping herself around to face us. I do like the look of that uniform. I wonder how I'd look in it.

Taylor makes a fist and socks it into his open palm. He shifts back and forth. "Can't say," he says.

"Wait a minute, wait a minute," I say. "I might have it on my phone. Remember when I took that picture out the car window?" I want to say to Luna: When you called me an idiot!

"Let's check it out," Sherry says, her hand out for my phone.

Taylor and I scrunch up our faces.

"Don't tell me—"

"That was my old phone. But they transferred all the photos."

And Luna breaks the news to her. We guess where the phone might be. Sherry finally says, "We have to look for it."

"What if he's there?" I say.

"We'll drive on by," Sherry says. "And we'll have four pairs of eyes on that license plate." And then she goes down the hall, real quick, saying, "I need my civvies. I shouldn't go out there without a partner, but this seems urgent." She comes out lickety-split in jeans and sweatshirt. She leaves her gun behind.

Taylor drives with Sherry beside him. The subdivision where Bony and Creep-ola live isn't far. On the way Sherry explains that we'll have to go down to the police station and report everything officially.

"You're okay with that?" she says to Taylor.

"I'm into it now," he says.

She explains that she wants to get the license plate number, if possible, or at least the state where the truck is registered. "If we know the state we can narrow the search."

I say, "Why can't you just arrest him?"

Taylor says, "Bet you need a search warrant—right?"

"And we can't get that," Sherry says, "unless there's probable cause."

"Us saying it isn't enough?" Luna says what I'm thinking. It's the same old story: what people our age think doesn't really count for much. I am so sick of being fourteen.

But Sherry surprises me and says, "That's hearsay and it might be enough. Might even be enough for a sneak-and-peek warrant, which is essentially what you all did. You sneaked in and got some evidence."

Luna and I peek at each other and grin. I think about that plastic library card Taylor used to break into Mr. Creep's house. I promise myself I'll never go anywhere without my plastic library card.

"But still," Sherry says, "We'll have to make it official at the station."

We are coming up on the house. For the first time, all sorts of people are out on the street. A woman hauling mulch to a tree in a wheelbarrow does not even glance our way. Two little boys on bikes. A man walking a fluffy white dog.

"This is good," Sherry says. "We won't be noticed."

"Creep's not there," Luna says. The driveway is empty.

Taylor tells Sherry about how we hid down the side street with pine trees all around. She decides that's a good plan. Taylor parks again in the direction of a quick getaway. He and Luna agree to stay with the car and Sherry and I search for my phone.

We walk through the woods and right into Mr. Creep's yard. "My phone's got a pink Body Glove," I say. She says we have to switchback through the brown grass and weeds, heads down. We each take a section of yard. When Sherry finishes hers, she moves off in the direction of the backyard next door. She slithers behind the storage shed. A woman comes out of the house. She's old, with gray hair, and she wears shorts and a t-shirt. Her knees are doughy and wrinkled. Ditto, her face. I listen to Sherry lie to her.

"My kids were playing in those trees the other day. One of them lost her cell phone."

The old woman says, "My dog found it."

Oh, I was so afraid she'd say that her dog ate it!

"That's a relief," Sherry says.

In a gentle, eager voice, the old woman says, "Won't you come in?" Sherry waves me over. The woman leads us around to the side of the house that faces away from Bony's house. We go inside the screened-in porch. A large quilt hangs on one wall. A yappy dog no bigger than a loaf of bread comes skittering out to the porch. "He won't hurt you," she says.

As if. I scoop the dog right up and he licks my face and wriggles back to the floor, tail wagging.

The old woman goes to a shelf and there's my phone, chewed up along one edge but still in one piece. I want to open the photos right then, but Sherry puts out her hand and lies again: "Hey, kiddo," she says, pretending to be my mother. I slap the phone into her hand, pretending to be sulky.

I am dying to open that phone and see if I have a good shot of Mr. Creep's license plate. Sherry is thanking the woman and the woman says, "Won't you two have some lemonade?" Sherry tries to be sweet and polite and say no. Right then we hear the Dodge Ram crunch into the driveway. Big red pickup. We can see it but because of the screening, I do not think Mr. Creep can see us. The screen makes everything outside look smoky.

Sherry shifts gears. She says, "Oh, look, peanut—" She's calling me *peanut*, like I am her baby girl and have been forever. "That's a lovely quilt," she says. "Did you make it?"

The woman says yes.

Sherry tucks the cell phone into her jeans. "I've always wanted to make a quilt."

Out of the corner of my eye I spy Creep-ola getting out of the pickup. He slams the door. He come around and opens Bony's door. He picks her up like a toddler and carries her on his hip.

Sherry and the old woman chatter away about quilts. Sherry says, "We'd like to see your quilts, wouldn't we, peanut?"

"Sure," I say. Is lying a good trait if I want to be a cop?

The woman invites us from the porch into the house. When we get inside to the messy kitchen, which smells like brownies, Sherry changes her mind about me. She says, "Go out the front door. Go tell Daddy I'll be there in a minute. Tell him to pull around to the front of the house."

"You want me to go?"

"Yes, peanut."

The old woman is so excited, talking about her quilts and their patterns. Wedding Ring. Log Cabin. "Skedaddle," Sherry says to me.

I hesitate at the front door. I glance back at Sherry as she steps into the woman's bedroom. She's looking back at me over her shoulder. She jerks her head at me. She doesn't have to say a word. I am her Peanut for now and I dart out into sunshine.

The Dodge Ram is parked at just the right angle. The license has a big Georgia peach on it—but I cannot make out the number. By now, I know enough not to make assumptions. Mr. Creep might be from Georgia and he might not. License plates are stolen every day. If he'd steal a girl, he'd be capable of stealing a license plate. I stumble through the woods, my heart hammering. The woods are wet and sticker bushes snag on my jacket. But right ahead is the Rambler and Taylor at the wheel. Luna leans against the hood, one knee cocked, her foot up on the bumper, her arms folded impatiently. She gives me a frown through her hair, which she's pulled down over one eye.

"Get in," I say. We hop into the backseat.

"What's up?" Taylor says, starting the engine.

"They came back!"

"Close call!"

"Sherry said to pick her up in front of the neighbor's."

Luna says, "And the phone?"

"Got it! And that's not all."

It takes less than a half-minute to pull up in front of the neighbor's house. I lean over the backseat and open Sherry's door. This has to be a sneaky getaway, not a quick getaway. She must have been watching for us because she comes out the front door. Even though she needs to hurry, she shakes hands with the woman. I'm sure she's thanking her for getting out the quilts.

"She's nice," I say.

Taylor says, "A nice cop."

Luna says, "So what else?"

"You'll see."

Sherry pops into the front seat and we take off, turning left instead of right, the way we'd come. Taylor says, "I can get us back to the main road."

"Well, *what*?" Luna says.

"Georgia peach," Sherry and I say, grimly. We say it exactly the same. Ordinarily we'd probably laugh at that. But not now. There's nothing to laugh about now.

"So he's from Georgia?" Taylor says.

"Maybe, maybe not," Sherry says.

"Just like we don't know if they're related or not," Luna says.

"Those ears are an awful lot alike," Taylor says.

Taylor and Luna seem to be thinking about how a girl might look like her dad. I sure don't want Mr. Creep to be her dad. Maybe my intuition has been just a little off. One thing I know for sure: Bony is in danger. I keep picturing that cage. Her fancy underpants folded beside it. But I don't want to think a dad would do that. We hit the main road and Taylor keeps to the speed limit.

Sherry pulls my phone out of her pocket and hands it back to me. "See if you got the license plate."

Luna and I click through the photos stored on my phone and there it is: half the license plate: EE3. I pass the phone to Sherry.

"That'll help," she says.

"Where to, Madam?" Taylor says.

Sherry says, "The station. I'll tell you where to turn."

"Oh, I know where to turn," Taylor says.

"Why's that?"

"I just make it my business," Taylor says.

That's when Luna's phone rings.

"It's Mama!"

"Answer it," Taylor says.

"Hiya." She puts the phone on speakerphone.

"Where are you two?" Kat says.

"With Dad," Luna says. I guess she doesn't feel like lying anymore.

"What's going on?" Kat sounds completely freaked out. Which can't be good for the baby. Can it? And being on speakerphone makes it seem like she has bronchitis, her voice raspy.

Taylor says, "Here, let me talk to her."

Luna says, "I'm putting Dad on."

Kat says, "No, don't—"

But then Taylor cuts in and says, "Kathy."

"Don't *Kathy* me," she says.

I did not know that she used to be called Kathy. It gives me a completely different view of her. She was a Kathy. Just like I used to be called Nikki. And before that, my mother called me Nicole. I was a different person then. Another life.

Kat says, "Put Luna back on."

"You need to listen to me," Taylor says. "To me and these girls."

"Where *are* you?"

"At the cop shop."

He glances at Sherry, who rolls her eyes, waiting for the phone call to end. She clicks through the photos on my cell phone. It's evidence now. I might never see it again. On the one hand, that's thrilling, but I need a cell phone. I need to know if those tweeting girls have their claws out yet.

"What's going on?" Kat worries, almost a shriek.

Luna slumps her shoulders and sighs. Her cheeks are blotchy. She's embarrassed. It bothers me, too, Sherry seeing our family troubles. What a rollercoaster, what a day. We will be grounded for months. Or longer. And this is the moment I realize without a doubt that Taylor is part of our blended family. What will the baby call him? So much for ordinariness. We will never go back to ordinariness.

"Calm down," Taylor says.

"Don't tell me to calm down," Kat says. She's almost growling. A mama bear.

"Well, why don't you come down here and see for yourself?"

"I'm on my way," Kat says.

Chapter 18

LUNA

W e've got to move on this right away," Sherry says. "If ya'll are right, she's in danger. Can't let it continue a moment longer."

Dad says, "Your mom'll find us at the station."

The police station is a brown brick building, not the kind of place you'd ever notice if there weren't tons of cop cars parked in the gated lot in back. Sherry directs us to park in front because Dad's driving, and technically we're visitors. She hops right out, slams her car door with a good wham, and marches off towards the front entrance. Dad follows her, a little too casually. Nick, on the sidewalk waiting for me, frowns and smiles at the same time, and I know she's as nervous and thrilled as I am.

A big white SUV is parked right beside Dad's Rambler, and two officers, a man and a woman, both wearing blue plastic gloves, have removed one of the tires and are squatted down, peering up into the rim. An open black suitcase, like an evidence collecting kit, sits on the pavement beside them. It's like *Dateline* and *48 Hours* up close! I wish I could ask them what they're looking for, but they don't even glance up, and Dad and Sherry are expecting us.

Inside, the police station looks like any other boring office building, not new and not old, the décor shades of brown, but the people who work there don't look boring or ordinary. The men and women who pass us in the hall wear khakis and polo shirts or black uniforms. They are strong and fit and move with energy and purpose, like Sherry. They greet Sherry and give us the once over.

Dad keeps his head down, and I don't blame him. I feel guilty, even though I haven't even done anything wrong. Not true—I've jaywalked. Skateboarded on city streets. Snuck into the Frost Fair. Shoplifted with Renda. Had sex and I'm not even sixteen. Would have it again if I got the right offer. Broke into Mr. Creep's house.

One of these no-nonsense, well-trained cops could detect guilt on my face. I know this fear's ridiculous, but it persists. Fascinating as this place is, I'll be relieved when we get out of here. I prefer my cops on TV.

When the first elevator arrives to take us to the second floor, the door slides open to reveal that there are already three cops in it, as well as a jittery looking man in handcuffs. I'm a little disappointed when Sherry indicates we'll wait for the next elevator.

Sherry doesn't have a real office, only a cubicle among many others. All around us are the muffled sounds of phones ringing, people chatting with each other or talking in an official manner on the phone. Somebody used too much cleaning product. Ugh.

But Sherry's cubicle's a whole different story. It's like going into an aquarium.

"Very cool," Dad says, and Nick and I agree.

The walls are covered with posters and photographs of underwater life, colorful and peaceful and stimulating at the same time. On her desk, a dark purple beta fish flutters and darts about in a little bowl. Gary, Sherry told us his name is. Yeah, she says, she took most of the photos. Fulty, our photography teacher, taught her well.

I bend closer to a small photograph tacked to the cubicle wall, one of a woman in a wet suit and scuba gear deep underwater, feeding something to a yellow and green tropical fish. "Great picture," I say. "Is that you? Where is this?"

By now Sherry is already sitting at her computer, booting it up, her back to us. "St. Barts," she says. "Scuba diving is my one true love. Other than my job."

"What about your honey? What happened to him?"

Did Dad really ask her that?

She shrugs. "Nothing happened to him. He's just not my one true love."

"That's good," Dad says and gives a weird little chuckle. God, how embarrassing.

Sherry's pretty and interesting, no doubt about that, but Dad and a police officer? That would be like a Nazi dating a nun. Sort of. He pulls a chair up beside Sherry, and Nick pulls one up on the other side.

I stand behind them, leaning on Dad's shoulders, maybe to remind him I'm there and keeping a close eye on him. Dad smells like Bay Rum with an underlayer of cigarettes. "What're you looking at?" I ask Sherry.

"National database for missing and exploited children," she explains. "We'll start here. We can run a check on his license plate later. Finding the kid's the most important thing."

It's beyond disturbing seeing the color photos of smiling children, all ages, all races, children who had no idea when the pictures were being taken that one day they would end up on a nightmare website such as this.

"Do you use this website as part of your job?" Nick asks Sherry.

"No, but anyone can use it," she says. "I'm on the cop squad," she goes on, tapping at her keyboard. "Crowd control. But we'll get some Special Victims people in on this soon as we have something to show them."

We search by state, looking at all the white girls who've disappeared in the last 10 years, starting in Florida and moving on.

We look at girls age fifteen and younger, just to be safe. Most of the missing kids are runaways or non-custodial parent abductions. Sherry has to explain how a parent could kidnap his or her own child.

"But maybe the kid's happier with the one that kidnapped her," I say, staring at a picture of a spiky haired girl wearing a cowboy shirt that she'd buttoned all the way up, her eyes not looking directly into the camera.

"That's a possibility," Sherry says. "But usually they don't have custody for a reason."

"I feel so bad for these kids," Nick says.

At this point Mama slips into the cubicle and the person who escorted her scoots away. Mama wears a leather jacket and her painting jeans and what I call her cozy shirt. Her face is tense. I want to hug her, but I'm scared. How mad is she going to be? Will she fly off the handle? We deserve to be chewed out. We lied big time. We took her away from working at the Sha. And we're with Dad.

I'm poised to defend us, but she bends down and kisses me and then Nick on the cheek, and then, without saying anything, slips out of her jacket. She moves up beside me to watch the computer screen with the rest of us. Absently she pats Dad's shoulder and, without looking at her, he squeezes her hand and lets it go.

As screwed up and frustrating and unreliable as Dad is, Mama has always allowed me to spend time with him when he does show up. I've never once worried about him kidnapping me. Am I wise or just näive? How'd we know he'd never kidnap me? Was it because he didn't love me enough? That seems crazy.

We all focus on the computer screen. How can there be *so many* missing kids? Where did they all go? And not one of them, as far as we can tell, is Bony, which isn't her real name. I never considered the fact the she might've been kidnapped as a baby... those sweet pictures of missing babies are the hardest ones to look at. If she's been with Mr. Creep for years...unthinkable. Many baby photos are matched up with weird, scary computer generated pictures of what the babies would probably look like today.

I worry that we might not recognize her.

We scroll through picture after picture, page after page, state after state. When the page for Virginia comes up, Nick and I point and say, "That's her."

Sherry clicks and brings up her poster. I want to study it but at the same time feel panicky to rush right out and find her. In the picture her face is plumper and rosier and she's really smiling and her hair, in a thick braid that hangs over her shoulder, is deep brown and shiny. She wears tiny gold balls in her ears. Her name is Isabella Rose Mathews. She's nine. Missing since September from Roanoke, Virginia. Circumstances: Non-custodial abduction.

By this point Nick and I jump up and down, saying again and again, "That's her! That's her!" and then, for some reason, we hug each other. Mama hugs both of us, too. Sherry keeps saying, "Are you absolutely sure?" Trying to bring us back down to earth.

Dad produces my camera and we compare before and after pictures. "You did it," he says. "Good work, girls." Dad is the first one who says it. I won't forget that.

Sherry scoots her chair back and rises up in one quick motion. "Ya'll sit tight. I'm going to go round up some of the team for a quick meeting."

The next day. January 3rd. 11:45 a.m.—maybe a future episode of *Dateline*! I know I shouldn't be thinking that, but I can't help it. Mostly I'm just thrilled that at last Mr. Creep will be arrested.

The Alligator Farm has a healthy holiday crowd. We're there, too, ready and waiting. Nick and I wear huge sunglasses and dorky oversized souvenir hats that we've purchased from the gift shop. Last night Mama helped Nick dye her hair electric blue as part of her disguise.

Mama and Dad and Jimmy and Nana Fanny sit at one of the metal tables across from the empty birdcage. Like strangers to me, Mama and Jimmy are disguised: Mama in a floppy hat and enormous sunglasses; Jimmy in a blonde Rod Stewart wig I wore for Halloween last year. They eat dishes of ice cream, pretending to be good friends out for an enjoyable afternoon of watching captive reptiles devouring repulsive rodents. I love seeing all my peeps together.

Nick and I were supposed to sit and eat ice cream with them, but we can't stay still. We keep agitating to get up and walk around, and finally Jimmy says, "Just *stay away* from the trouble. No going anywhere near the snack bar or the birdcage. Understand?"

We promise. It wasn't easy to convince Mama to let us be at the Farm when it all went down, but Dad, and later Jimmy, persuaded her that it would be okay—we deserved it because of our persistence on Isabella's behalf.

And Sherry said it was okay, since there will be lots of other people there. When Nana Fanny found out about the plans, she insisted upon coming, too.

Morris Ashe and Isabella, Morris Ashe and Isabella—their real names. I can't wrap my mind around that, living a fake life. Mason wasn't even his real name. And Isabella is actually his niece! They'll be here soon. Five cops hang out in strategic locations around the alligator pit, two of them together like a couple, the other three scattered about. Just like us, they're pretending to look casual. To me they look anything but. It seems to me that anyone with half a brain can tell they're cops, even though they're wearing jeans and t-shirts and sunglasses like every other person. Sherry assured me that they're armed and fitted with bullet-proof vests underneath their shirts. But more than likely, she said, they won't need either the guns or vests. Let's hope.

Because of the warm sunshine, the Alligator Farm stinks of animal poop and muck—more than usual. What will it be like in summer? I'll never know, because I'll never set foot here again after today. Nick and I cruise the perimeter, pretending to study the alligators and reptiles as long as we can stand it before we swivel to see if our quarry has arrived. The oblivious crowd of tourists who laugh and cavort and whine have no idea what's going down, but the parrots squawk extra loud like they feel the tension in the air.

In addition to the cops inside the Farm, there are four officers out in the parking lot who, as soon as Mr. Creep—he'll always be Mr. Creep to me—and Isabella come in, will guard the exits so that he can't leave. That's their plan.

It's so cool that Nick and I helped them come up with the plan. Between then and now, they'd stationed officers in an unmarked car outside Mr. Creep's house just in case he decided to go off on a joy ride in the middle of the night. But late this morning Sherry called and told us that he hadn't, and that we were going with the Alligator Farm plan.

Finally the big clock above the snack bar reads noon. What if they don't come? What if this is the *one day* they don't come? Molly, who's got no idea what's going on—in the meeting yesterday they advised us not to tell her—climbs into the pit with her stick, turns on her mic and starts dishing out facts about alligators in her official, cheery voice, like she hasn't done it a million times before.

Finally Mr. Creep and Isabella appear, walking through the crowd toward his favorite bench. His black sunglasses hide his hard eyes and his head bobs around like a bobblehead, like he's checking everyone out. I hardly ever pray, but I pray right then. I pray he won't notice that anything's different. Isabella, dolled up in another short dress, her hair curled and pouffed out, fixes her eyes on the ground. And I wonder, who fixes her hair? I want to rush up and grab her myself, but instead, Nick and I, both shaky, drop down onto a bench and pretend to be listening to an iPod with one set of headphones, something we planned earlier. There isn't actually any music playing, but we nod our heads like there is. We barely slept the night before.

I wish so badly that TJ were here holding my hand. I'd feel calmer. He's always been on our side. I can't wait to tell him about this.

Mr. Creep leads his captive to their bench in front of the empty birdcage. The alligator show goes on, but Nick and I can't look at anything except them. It's almost over, I whisper, over and over. I can't help it.

Mr. Creep seems to be muttering to Isabella while she stares at a nearby sable palm. Now that I know her name, and where she's from, I'm starting to think of her as a real person, a person who happens, temporarily, to be in this horrible situation. But she used to have a normal life. Is that what she's thinking about? Her parents? Does she miss them? Does she have brothers and sisters? She must have a best friend. Was she a Girl Scout? A troublemaker? A swimmer or a gymnast? Did she love Justin Beiber? *The Diary of a Wimpy Kid*? Was she a good student? What's it like in Roanoke, Virginia? I have no idea—I've never been there—but could she ever forget it? The way the trees looked, the sunlight, the buildings downtown. Her house, her street, her yard, her school. Maybe she had a dog, or a cat, or a beta fish. And she hadn't been home for Christmas. She'd told Nick and me, "He's all I got." She might've given up hope by now, hope that she'd ever get her old life back.

The alligator show is done. People applaud. The gators crunch their reward rodents and Molly climbs out of the pit and disappears into the EMPLOYEES ONLY office attached to the snack bar. She hasn't noticed us. People start milling around again.

I can't breathe, waiting for Mr. Creep to leave for the popcorn. Get up, damn you. *Get up get up get up*, Nick and I start chanting in a whisper. If he doesn't get up things might get violent. The cops will still approach Mr. Creep and Isabella and take her away, but who knows what he'll do then? And there's the hunting rifle in his truck. It'd be so much simpler, and safer, to snatch her while his back is turned.

The Creep doesn't move. He stubbornly sits. The two of them

are like planted there. He says something to Isabella, taps her on the head. She ignores him. Mr. Fucking Creep. Morris Fucking Ashe. What made him do such a thing? Did he just wake up one morning and think, "Maybe I'll kidnap my niece today and keep her in a cage so I can rape her whenever I want! Sounds like fun to me!" Doesn't he have a job? A family? What happened to the drunk, suntanned woman and the other kid?

I glance over at my own family's table. They've given up the pretense of eating and are staring fixedly at Mr. Creep. The officers scattered around are a bit more subtle. One large guy with a shaved head, over by the entrance, is "studying" a brochure, the man and woman "couple" behind the bird cage are "observing" some tropical birds, and another woman, in walking shorts and hiking boots, leans on a railing, texting someone. The soccer mom nearest Mr. Creep and Isabella is jabbering on a cell phone. The crowd thins and still the two of them don't move.

Now Mr. Creep seems to be gazing right at Nick and me. Does he know what's up? Does he recognize us? Nick and I are clutching at each other and swaying to the pretend music and I can feel my pulse racing at a sickening speed. This is all our fault. Nick and I told them that Mr. Creep *always* got popcorn. They were counting on him to get popcorn.

The officer with the brochure glances at his watch.

Nana Fanny rises to her feet. What the hell? She's been briefed, told to stay put, but she's a wild card. She's never one to do as she's told. She swishes along in her hippie skirt and a pink t-shirt, big straw bag slung over her shoulder, and heads toward the snack bar but walks right on past. Where on earth is she going? I have the horrible urge to bust out laughing. Mama, Daddy and Jimmy gape at her. I can tell they have no idea either.

"Oh no," Nick murmurs. "Oh no oh no oh no."

Nana Fanny is now in front of Mr. Creep. She is, believe it or not, talking to him! She removes a camera from her straw bag and gestures over to my family's table. Is she really asking him to take their picture? Morris Ashe, child abductor, wanted by the FBI? She is.

All the officers seem poised to pounce.

Mr. Creep takes her camera and unfolds himself from the bench, not looking too happy about doing it. I can almost read his mind. Refusing to take an old lady's picture will make him seem even more suspicious than he already seems. Will Isabella go with him? He says something to her and she nods and stays put, thank God, and then he follows Nana Fanny over to where Mama and Daddy and Jimmy are sitting—frozen, it looks like, in disbelief. As they walk, Nana Fanny chats with the dangerous criminal as if they were two tourists swapping tips about old Florida.

Nana Fanny sits down next to Jimmy, who wraps his arm around her like he'll never let go, then they all squish together with big fake smiles on their faces. Mr. Creep has probably recognized them from Spudnuts. If he has, is he suspecting a trap? Oh Lordy. I shouldn't care about the picture, but I do. I can't wait to see the picture he's about to take. The expressions on their faces. It might be the best picture ever taken.

Mr. Creep raises the camera and, watching the screen, angles it just so.

Quicker than I thought anybody could move, the soccer mom officer and the officer "couple" sweep over to Isabella before Mr. Creep finishes snapping the picture.

Chapter 19

NICK

Louise is like: "Wow. This is major."

I say, "It is?"

"Indeed."

She's referring to all of it, everything that I've told her. The fire. The idea of the new baby, which even I know might not be the same as the reality of the new baby. Taylor. The sleepover. And capturing Isabella and the C. (I can no longer stand to say his name. I've squeezed him down to one letter—C.) I'm sitting in a comfy chair in Louise's small office. We have a view of the canal and rich people playing on their boats. Blue water, milk-white sails. It's almost a hot day.

Louise's wearing dangly earrings, all feathers and beads. Her hair is black and curlicues around her head. Her mouth in bright red lipstick is like a bow on a present. She says, "Think of where you were two weeks ago! You actually said you were bored and might run away."

"I did?"

She shuffles through a flowered notebook. She pokes a finger at one page: "Here it is. And I quote: 'I'm bored with this place. I might run away.'"

I stare out the window. I like that I can stare out the window and Louise will just sit there, patiently, no pressure. Finally I say, "Let's open the box."

"Are you ready?"

"I've waited six years."

I pick up my mother's wooden box. How huge this box felt to me when I was a little kid. Now it just fits on my lap.

I open the box. A smell like stale incense comes at me. A woodsy smell. Everything fits neatly inside, like a puzzle. For some reason, I sniff each thing. I squeeze shut my eyes and try to imagine my mother handling each thing. Choosing each thing. Making it fit in the box. Thinking of me. A white box with a silver friendship ring inside. A pincushion I made for her when I was in kindergarten. A red Swiss Army knife with a tag attached that reads *Grandpa Lonnie*. That was her dad who died in a war. There are two books: *The Mill on the Floss* and *A Tree Grows in Brooklyn*. Pink mittens she knit herself. At the bottom of the box is an envelope. On the outside, in what must be my mother's handwriting, it says: Letter for Nicole. In Case I Die Before My Time.

"I'm saving the letter," I say to Louise. "It's private."

"How do you feel now?"

"Relieved."

Louise waits. I can see by the digital clock on her bookcase that our fifty minutes are almost up.

I say, "And curious."

Louise doesn't budge. Distantly, I hear another client entering the outer office, clinking sugar into a cup of tea. I know I'm not finished, but I don't have much time.

"Loved," I finally say. "Like she loved me."

Louise gives me one of her bountiful smiles.

•

Dad picks me up and drops me at Nana Fanny's where I am staying the night. Luna starts her real driver's ed today. I can hardly believe I'll have a sister who can drive. I picture us together in a sporty car, while Kat and Dad stay home with the baby. Only two more days and school will start and my anonymous life at school might be—probably *will* be—be over. I'm not the same person I was two weeks ago. Nana's at the grocery, so I'm all alone in the house, just me and Haiku. I text her to see when she'll be back. *Under an hour,* she texts back. Time—I have time.

Haiku and I climb up into Nana's big bed. We get under an afghan that's like a rainbow. Haiku settles down, right next to my leg. I want everything just right for opening the letter. And everything at Nana Fanny's does feel just right. She's not renovating. Sunshine comes through the high window beside the bed and makes a gorgeous yellow shadow on the wall. The bed smells fresh, like vanilla. I am surrounded by family photos. There's one of my mother and father on their wedding day. He's got long hair that fit right in at the vinyl shop in Tallahassee. She's wearing a short white dress and a short white veil. With red shoes. I love those red shoes.

The letter starts off *Dear Nicole.* I am Nicole. And I am Nick. I am both those people. *If you are reading this, it means I'm gone. And gone before my time, before you grew up. On* Oprah *I saw a guy who said that all parents should write a letter like this and put it away, in case the unthinkable happens and you don't have the chance to say things to your children before you die. So I did. I wrote this when you were only three years old. You had a Cesarean birth. You can look this up. It means that the doctor made an incision in my tummy and you came out that way. I could see it in a mirror. You were a beautiful baby because you didn't have to struggle through the birth canal. But that also meant that you never went through the first struggle: being born. I always wonder if you will have struggles later in life becoming who you are. Of course, we all do. I have faith that you will become an amazing person. Right now, you are talking a blue streak and asking lots of questions. Sometimes I have to look up the answers. Your daddy and I go into your room every night to say goodnight a second time after you've gone to sleep. We hold hands and love you. He always says that you're the best thing he's ever done. If I'm no longer with you, I imagine you have a new family. You know why? Because your daddy is a great guy.*

Kat always says that, too.

If you have a new family I hope you let everyone in that family love you. Remember: Love's imperfect.

She must mean Luna.

But you can't turn your back on it. Here's another thing: you like to hide stuff. We find your stuffed panda in a special place in the kitchen. A down-low cupboard. We find your pacifiers tucked into an old patent leather purse I gave you. I want to tell you that it's okay to have secrets. It's part of growing up, learning what to keep to yourself and what to share.

Luna says that, too.

I try to picture you the way you are now. Do you still like shoes? You always want to change your shoes. Do you still like chocolate bunnies? Do you worry about animals? You told me when you were quite small that it wasn't right to eat them. Oh, Nicole, have a wonderful life. Be good to yourself and others. Love, Mom

I want this letter to never stop. I read it three times.

Later I go sit on the curb. It's still a warm day. I am hoping that Maeve will come out, and then I tell myself, "Why hope?" I get up and ring her screechy doorbell. Her mother lets me in, saying, "Maeve was restless. So glad you're here." She texts Maeve and she comes up the stairs from the basement and says, "Do you have your skateboard?"

"It was stolen." Habitual liar, that's me. "But I reported it."

"I have another you can use."

So we go skateboarding in the street once we realize Sherry must be at work. Maeve is really good. Ollies, kickflips. She's been skating since she was seven. I do all I can to keep from falling. She says, "You can get it. It just takes practice." For some reason, this makes me almost cry. She's encouraging, like a real friend. I start to tell her about Taylor saying, "Face your fear," but that seems so complicated, explaining who Taylor is. I'll tell her later. Nana comes home—ever cheerful—and waves to us, as if it's a perfectly normal thing for me to have a friend next door to her.

Later, Maeve and I sit on the curb. I tell her all about Isabella and C.

"We'll never see her again," I say. Except maybe on the cover of a magazine. All we know so far is that he's her uncle. And her parents let her go with him. What little I know, I know by heart, whether I want to or not. I imagine Isabella trying to smile. But the way I see it, her eyes look like she's not sure who she really is. It's a reminder to always keep my eyes wide open. Alert to trouble.

That first day—after the arrest—Dad took us all out for lunch at the Lovetree Café where I could get a veggie burrito. "I am so proud of Nana Fanny," I must have said ten times. And she said, "*Some*one had to do something." We re-played the high points, like a favorite song. Luna said, "Zow-ee, did you see the look on his face when they took a hold of him?" C's face was like a balloon with the air seeping out of it. Saggy.

"He just gave up," Dad said.

Taylor said, "Getting caught was probably a relief."

We tried to imagine what Isabella's reunion with her parents was like. Kat said that Isabella needs to be treated like a newborn baby. She needs to learn what love is. And yet, Sherry had said that her parents *let her go with him*. That worries me.

When they got her back, did they stay in a nice hotel? Did her mother give her a bath and wash her hair? Did they take her to Dillard's and buy her new outfits? Did they lie on the bed and hug for a long time? Maybe living with them will only be a little better than being in C's dog crate. I don't feel like much of a hero.

After the celebration lunch, Dad put Luna and me—his child laborers—to work. In spite of the smoke damage, the B had one room rented for that night. Opening night! Dad actually said, "The show must go on!" The front porch needed to be swept and leftover red brick pavers had to be carried to the garage out back. Luna and I hardly had a minute to talk. We passed each other going back and forth to the garage with gritty stacks of pavers. I could only carry two at a time, but Luna could carry four. I wondered: Would she always be stronger than I was? Once we stopped in the middle of the driveway. Luna's mouth screwed up like a radish rose. Then she said, "This is not the kind of work I want to do when I grow up."

I said, "Me, neither. I want to be like Sherry."

"Yeah, right. You think Jimmy'll let you be a cop?"

"You get to be what you want," I said.

Just then Kat opened the kitchen window and said, "In here, my chicklets. I have news for you."

We dusted ourselves off and went in the back door. She handed each of us a healthy muffin with carrot bits sticking out all over it. We sat down to eat. The kitchen had come together. It was homey, with one wall painted red. Ruffle-y curtains danced at the windows. She had some music on way low: a Motown girl group I didn't know the name of. Kat always says Motown is the best music to bake by.

"What's up?" Luna said.

Kat sat down and leaned across the table, her hands locked together, a serious look on her face. She said, "Reporters have been calling."

"For us?" I said.

She shook her head yes. "But you don't want that kind of notoriety."

"What's notoriety?" I said.

"When everyone else in the world knows what you've done. It'd make you vulnerable. We have to protect you."

Luna said, "Don't overdo it."

Kat said, "We don't want to talk to reporters."

"We don't?" I said.

"And another thing," Kat said. "At breakfast tomorrow? Wear nice clothes and mind your manners. Nana Fanny and Taylor and Sherry are coming to breakfast. We want the place to seem full."

"You want us to lie about how many people are staying here?" Luna said.

"Not *lie!*" Kat said. "Just be on your best behavior."

"You invited Dad?" Luna said. She didn't quite believe it.

I thought about the moment when Taylor and Kat had squeezed hands at the cop shop. I didn't feel bad toward him anymore; he had helped us so much.

"Yes, yes. And TJ and his father."

"Bethany would die if she knew," I said.

Squinching her eyes in an evil way, Luna said, "We might have to tell her."

Just then a happy little white dog scampered into the kitchen. I picked her up. A woman came waddling after, saying, "Princess, Princess!"

Dad stuck his head in the kitchen. He was wearing a shirt with the lyrics of a seafaring song on the front: *Cape Cod girls ain't got no combs. They brush their hair with codfish bones.* He introduced the woman. She was our first guest, but he didn't let her know that. He eased the woman and the dog back into the hall and then to the foyer, where he explained the house to her and her husband. We could hear his spiel from the kitchen. In a jolly voice, he told the husband about the pirate sing at a nearby tavern. He stacked their luggage in the dumbwaiter, saying, "It's a newfangled, labor-saving device."

"But Jimmy said *no dogs!*" Luna whispered.

"He changed his mind," Kat said.

"That's what minds are for," I said.

Luna and Kat looked at me strangely.

I said, "That's a direct quote. From Nana Fanny."

Kat said, "He's going to decide on a case-by-case basis."

I was already daydreaming about all the dogs I would get to know at the B between that moment and the time I went away to college. Six years times maybe 200 dogs a year. Wow.

Back at the garage, I said to Luna, "Talking to reporters might be fun. You want to be on *Dateline*."

"Don't you get it? Keep your mouth shut," she said, "or we'll never solve another crime as long as we live. Act ordinary. Just act ordinary."

I said I wouldn't tell anyone, but I tell Maeve everything. She listens. A few times she says, "Wow." And "That was brave of you." I show her the friendship ring my mom put in the box. I'll wear it forever. I tell Maeve the whole story and on one level I really want her to approve of what we did for Bony, but on another very practical level, I want her to spread the word. To protect me. Should I feel ashamed of that?

Breakfast starts at eight. Luna and I wake early and put on dresses. She says I look a little like the murderer Rosemary in the old photo. I step into the hallway right then and take down the photo and put it in a drawer in the built-in cupboards. That photo had hung there for a gazillion years. But no more. "Don't talk about them," I tell her. I am finished with ghosts. My real life is scary enough.

Everyone is there at the table.

TJ's hair has been combed. His dad wears a white shirt and a tie. Sherry's in a red dress with a scoop neckline. Nana Fanny is all flowery. Dad has an apron tied tight around his waist and he shuttles back and forth from the long dining room table to the kitchen, humming pirate songs, helping Kat. Coffee is on the sideboard, with juices and teas. Dad's rock and roll stuff that he's collected for years has finally found a home. Framed sheet music and signed photos of Roy Orbison and the Supremes. We have *Sha-Na-Na Let's Go to the Hop* mugs. The guests chatter away about their road trip up from Miami. Everything is cozy and as it should be.

Oops.

Everything but that empty place where Luna's dad is supposed to sit.

TJ has saved places for us. He's perched the American Girl Roller Derby Queen on a seat next to him. He pats the chair and says, "Luna—this one's for you." But Luna says, "I'm not hungry." Not even that doll can change her mood.

She disappears into the foyer. I sit down on one side of TJ and try to act normal. Nana Fanny silently picks up her napkin and demonstrates properly laying it back on her lap. So I unfurl my napkin and rest it on my lap. The dog named Princess is upstairs. I feel tongue-tied.

"There's a News3 JAX van out there," Luna says. "And a guy with a camera!"

"Uh-oh," Nana Fanny says, but she goes ahead and takes a goopy bite of warm cinnamon roll. Like it's really no big deal.

I'm excited—maybe I want to be on TV.

Sherry says, "I'll handle this."

That's when I realize the grown-ups have discussed it. Sherry is assigned the duty of getting rid of the media so that the show can go on. She struts out the front door. Even though she's in high heels and that red dress, she seems like she could breath fire.

I ask to be excused, and I'm into the foyer before Dad can say, "Young lady! Nicole!" Just playing his part. He doesn't have the time to discipline me. That will always be in our favor now that we live at the Sha-Na-Na Bed and Breakfast.

I stand beside Luna and we watch out the side window, our heads close together. Sherry meets the cameraman on the sidewalk. He places a gigantic paper coffee cup on the grass, like he plans to camp out there.

"Awesome camera," I say to Luna, wanting to distract her.

"It's okay."

A woman reporter in a yellow suit that looks like an oven mitt comes waltzing up behind the cameraman. Sherry sticks out her arm to stop them. We can't hear what she says, but the woman reporter twists up her face and gets mad. Sherry folds her arms, blocking the way.

Luna says, "Dad's gone."

"He might come back."

"I know." She's sadder than ever, but she makes fun of herself and lets out a fake cry like a baby doll: "Waahh!"

"Girls!" Nana Fanny says sternly.

I loop my arm through Luna's. We have this electric connection. "You know," I tell her, "they don't really need us here." It is the truth. The grown-ups (and even TJ) are happy to drink coffee and tell stories on themselves. "Let's ditch these dresses and go sit in the car."

We don't even stay to see what happens with the News3 JAX people. We race upstairs and change our clothes. Luna stealthily slips the car keys into her pocket.

Behind the house we get into Kat's Subaru. Oh, we're about to break a big rule. We wait until we think Sherry is back indoors. Luna starts the car. She's wearing a baseball cap and I duck down as she pulls out of the driveway. No one will spot us.

We ride around the block. "This is so cool," I say. And then: "If I got rescued, I'd want a mom who goes around the house at night to make sure all the doors and windows are locked. And caramel corn. I'd want that, too."

Luna says, "If I got rescued, what I'd want is a dad who'd teach me something. Anything."

"'Like how to open a locked door with a library card?"

"Exactly."

We make a list of what we'd want if we were saved from living in a cage.

I say, "We have to keep our intuition sharp."

Luna stops at the playground, and we sit in the swings like little kids. A silver car pulls up near us. An expensive car. I don't know how I know that, but I do. A car that has been polished and waxed. With a chrome grill as bright as a movie star's smile. Bethany climbs out of the car and comes over to Luna. Bethany's mother gets all prissy and waits near the picnic table and lights a cigarette. Disgusting. She and Bethany wear the exact same outfit: black velvet pants and animal print tops and sunglasses.

"Bethany," Luna says.

"Come over to my house," Bethany says. "We can get online."

Luna might be tempted. If she goes to Bethany's house, she might never have to worry about whether she is welcome at a certain table in the lunchroom. She might never have to feel lost at our new school.

Before Luna can answer, Bethany says, in a snotty voice: "Nick—where'd you get those clothes?" She giggles, like I'm not supposed to feel bad. I hate when people insult you and then say, "Just kidding."

Luna reaches over and puts her arm around my shoulder. "Don't you ever talk that way to my sister."

"Oh, now she's your sister?" Bethany says, a threat in her voice. I think she's trying to tell Luna that she'll pay for this. That it isn't over.

Bethany's mom stomps on her cigarette and they return to the expensive car and peel off. Were they trolling for a friend for Bethany? Someone to keep her entertained while the mom did what she wanted? Luna and I don't have to worry about that. We can make other friends, but we will always have each other. Their license plate is the kind you can order special: FLFOX. Florida Fox. That's part of my secret job now: to memorize license plates. Notice details. Pay attention.

"They're kind of scary," I say.

Luna's arm drops away from my shoulder, but how it makes me feel doesn't go away. Protected. I wish that Luna had known my mom.

She says, "Face your fear!"

We laugh so hard I think I might wet my pants. Finally that stops and we fall quiet, peaceful in the January sunshine, just sitting on the picnic table. Luna says, "This holiday break went by fast."

"Do you think we could send her a present or something?" Luna knows that I mean Isabella. Maybe I can send her something from the box my mother left me.

"I doubt it," Luna says. Then: "Well, maybe."

I like the sound of the car doors thwacking shut when we leave. "Thrills and spills," Luna says, real softly, like she is singing. I love the gritty sound of our wheels on the asphalt. We can go anywhere, do anything.

On the curb in front of Nana's, Maeve listens to the story of what really mattered the last two weeks. She's cool in her skater girl clothes—high-top sneakers she sequined herself, gray velvet leggings, a neon hoodie. The sky feels perfect—winter blue with peppy clouds. On some level I'm thinking about those two books in my mother's box, wondering which one I'll read first. There are so many things ahead of me. I'm blathering on, but Maeve doesn't seem to mind.

"Did you get caught?" she says. "Driving, I mean."

"Not this time," I say.

Maeve laughs. She gets it. She gets *me*. I don't have to say, "We will break more rules. We will undoubtedly get caught someday."

And then we go into Maeve's house to make brownies.

About the Authors

Elizabeth Stuckey-French is the author of two novels, *The Revenge of the Radioactive Lady* and *Mermaids on the Moon*, as well as a collection of short stories, *The First Paper Girl in Red Oak, Iowa*. With Janet Burroway and Ned Stuckey-French, she is the editor of *Writing Fiction: A Guide to the Narrative Craft*, a popular creative writing textbook. She teaches at Florida State University.

Patricia Henley is the author of four story collections—including *Other Heartbreaks*—and two novels, *In the River Sweet* and *Hummingbird House*, which was a finalist for the National Book Award. She taught at Purdue University for 27 years.